UN

'Arsenic?' Richard said. 'Poison? Then it has
confirmed what you suspected, Doctor? My father
was poisoned?'

'Yes,' the doctor answered with a tremendous
expression of gravity. 'Yes, I regret to tell you that
there can be no doubt. I found arsenic in your
father's body after carrying out my tests more than
once, and its presence absolutely confirmed my
diagnosis at the time of his death. It was not due to
natural causes.'

'I must therefore ask you, sir,' Inspector
Redderman added quietly, 'to accompany me to
the police office . . .'

Also by Evelyn Hervey in Sphere Books:
THE GOVERNESS

The Man of Gold

H. R. F. KEATING

writing as

EVELYN HERVEY

SPHERE BOOKS LIMITED

First published in Great Britain by
George Weidenfeld & Nicolson Limited 1985
Copyright © 1985 by Evelyn Hervey
Published by Sphere Books Ltd 1986
27 Wrights Lane, London W8 5TZ

Set in Times

Printed and bound in Great Britain by
Cox & Wyman Ltd, Reading

Chapter One

Even before the terrible events of the spring of the year '74 Miss Unwin had regretted, frequently and sometimes bitterly, her decision to accept the post of governess to Mr Richard Partington's two motherless girls. On the very day she had first gone to call on Mr Partington at his father's grim old house in the Harrow Road on the western outskirts of London she had done her utmost to decline the position.

Yet she had accepted it. She had known almost from the moment she had seen the twins, so thin and forlorn in their bedraggled frocks with the scanty drooping unstarched flounces, that she would agree to come to them.

At the time, though she hardly realised it, it was not only the challenge which the two warily suspicious girls, so startlingly alike in looks, presented to her that made her act so against her customary common sense. There had been something else. An attraction, she knew not of what nature, had made her determined to go to the house.

Certainly the remuneration offered did nothing to make her feel she ought to accept the post.

'As to salary,' Mr Richard Partington had said, giving her a sudden wry, apologetic smile, there and gone in a moment, 'as to salary the figure fixed upon is twenty-five pounds per annum.'

He must have seen the expression of dismay Miss Unwin had struggled in vain to conceal. The sum was barely half what she received in her present post, soon to come to an end.

'That is – That is –' Mr Partington at once stammered. 'That is twenty-five pounds is the sum which my father, from whose purse your salary will be found, is prepared to offer.'

He came to a halt then and his round face was lit up by another of the rueful quick smiles Miss Unwin was to come to know so well.

'And I am afraid I am instructed to say,' he added, 'that he will not budge from that figure.'

At that moment Miss Unwin had had words of uncompromising refusal on her lips. It was monstrous, really monstrous, to be asked to accept less than some servants. But the two little girls, standing so silently looking at her like a pair of identical kittens ready at a moment's fright to dart away, had kept those words from being voiced. Or had there even then been something else? It was a question Miss Unwin was to come to ponder very frequently when winter had at last yielded to spring.

She turned at that moment to the girls and put another question to them, something merely designed to make them talk and reveal whether the spark of intelligence she thought she glimpsed behind their carefully unexpressive faces did truly exist.

'Now, girls, how old are you? Your Papa has not told me that.'

The twin who was standing an inch or so forward spoke up.

'We're nine.'

Their father hastily intervened.

'Louisa, Louisa, you should address this lady as Miss Unwin. It is not at all polite to do otherwise.'

Once more there darted out to Miss Unwin that elusive timid smile that seemed to contradict so entirely the plain, round face which at the same time it illuminated.

'So you are Louisa,' Miss Unwin said to the first twin, keeping firmly to the business in hand. 'And what is your sister's name?'

'It's Maria.'

But quickly Louisa's sister covered up her twin's renewed lack of politeness.

'I am Maria, Miss Unwin. And we had our ninth birthday just last week.'

'I see. And were you given some nice presents?'

'No,' said Louisa, sharply uncompromising. 'We had only one each.'

'But they were nice, Miss Unwin,' Maria again came to the rescue. 'They were spinning tops. A red one for Lou and a blue for me. Papa made them himself.'

Miss Unwin felt a rising up of surprise. The children of this house which, shabby though it seemed, was a gentleman's house, to be given as birthday presents no more than a homemade wooden top apiece. And nothing, so it appeared, from the grandfather who was to pay her own salary. It was strange. Strange indeed.

She decided that this was a subject that had better not be pursued. Her few words with the girls in any case had shown her that the spark of quickness she had wondered about did indeed exist, if in Louisa's case it took a form that was less than pleasant. But that made the challenge of putting things right all the more appealing.

She turned to the girls' father.

'The sum you suggest, sir,' she said, 'is less than I am receiving at present.'

'Yes, yes. I know it is small, terribly small. But – But, let me assure you, were it in my power – No. No, when it is in my power I shall remunerate you as handsomely as – As any Lord in the land would do.'

'I should not require a greater sum than my services are worth,' Miss Unwin said.

Mr Partington swung round, with an abruptness of action seemingly a compensation for his noticeably small stature, an abruptness Miss Unwin was to come to know as typical, and addressed his two daughters.

'Girls, girls. Beg this lady to accept. You know that

of all who have seen you she is –'

He paused and turned back to give Miss Unwin a look that was almost a frank stare.

'She is – She is the most kindly looking by far.' He gave her a different smile then, a sudden grin that spread from one side of his wide mouth to the other. 'And I am sure much the cleverest.'

'You have hardly had opportunity to judge of that, sir,' Miss Unwin said.

She had felt the need, the duty even, to state the truth. She was not going to yield to any obvious flattery, however warmly and pleasantly spoken.

And yet in the end she had yielded.

She did not do so there and then in the little chilly parlour where Mr Partington saw her, with its fire grate empty even on that grey wintry day and with its hard horsehair chairs and yet harder and more forbidding horsehair sofa. But, even as Mr Partington had seized up his hat to escort her out, she had known for all she said firmly that she would need a day and a night to make up her mind that she was going to accept.

Not even the ridiculous incident over summoning a cab put her off.

As she had stood on the wide pavement outside the old, paint-worn house next to the factory where Partington's Patent Pins, those useful devices that everybody knew of, were manufactured with the sharp wind tugging at her skirts, Mr Partington had insisted that she must have a cab to take her back to Bayswater.

'No, really, it is kind, but there is an omnibus that goes almost the whole way.'

'No, no, Miss Unwin. An omnibus for a lady who has come all this way to see me and my poor girls. I could not think of such a thing.'

'But I came on an omnibus, sir.'

'And it was not right that you should have done so. It was abominable that you should have done so. It was very

4

wrong of me not to have made it plain when I wrote that of course you should take a cab when you came here. At my expense. That is, at my father's –'

He came to a full stop and looked down at the grey stones of the pavement with such a disconsolate expression on his round countenance that Miss Unwin had been tempted to laugh. And had found in herself then somehow an even greater determination to take the offered post despite the meanness of the salary.

But before Richard Partington had been able to excuse himself any further a hansom had come clattering along on the far side of the road and, waving his hat like a madman, he had run into the roadway to halt it.

Yet this was not the end of the business. That came when Miss Unwin was sitting safely behind the half-doors which protected her from the cab's horse and the grime upthrown from the cobbles. Richard Partington attempted then to pay the driver perched up behind her on his box.

He plunged his hand into his pocket with the evident intention of pulling out a shilling for the fare. And, as evidently, he found his pocket empty. He tried then the other pockets in his much-worn green trousers, which yet showed a certain elegance of cut, as well as the pockets in his blue swallow-tail coat, as old, as elegantly fitting his short figure, but not really matching the green trousers.

Had this odd mixture of garments been a factor in Miss Unwin's irrational decision to take the poorly paid and unpromising post? Its air of being at once slightly ridiculous and yet of speaking of the trials of a widower's life had struck her certainly. But she did not really know.

The curiously dressed young widower having searched his each and every pocket and been unable to find as much as a sixpence, indeed not as much as a single farthing, looked up at her piteously.

'My dear Miss Unwin,' he said, 'I'm afraid I shall have

to ask you to pay the fellow yourself. Oh, but have you enough in your purse? If you haven't I'll – I'll – I'll manage somehow, see if I don't.'

'Pray, don't concern yourself, Mr Partington. I have quite sufficient. Don't concern yourself at all.'

What she had said was only partly true. She did have a shilling in her purse and three pennies besides. But that was all that she had allowed herself for the remainder of the week, and if the shilling was given to the cab-man there were things she would have to do without unless she was to rob her small savings.

But she put a brave face on it. She felt she could not mortify Richard Partington more than he had been mortified already.

So the hansom rolled smartly away and she sat there trying to persuade herself once again not to take the post. And knew that no amount of rational argument was going to be of any avail.

Somehow the poverty that seemed so evident in everything she had seen in the shabby house beside the pin works made her feel she could not do what, clearly, a good many applicants had done before her: leave in appalled dismay and forget the offer had ever been made.

The grim horsehair chairs and sofa in the little chilly parlour had not repelled her as they should have done in any sensible view of them. The very lack of a fire in the grate, however small and smoky, had not made her say to herself that the days she would spend in winter in the house would be cheerless in the extreme. The dinginess of the twins' white pinafores and the sad unstarched flounces of their frocks had only made her heart go out to them.

In her own earliest days, when the workhouse had been all she had known, she had endured worse deprivation by far. Then she had had nothing, and little hope of ever having anything. Richard Partington's daughters, on the other hand, or rather old Mr Partington's daughters, on the other hand, or rather old Mr Partington's granddaughters as it seemed, were deprived surely because the good things that could have been theirs had been deliberately withheld.

As the cab bowled along towards Bayswater she could not help thinking, too, with wonder and dismay about Richard Partington and the total lack of money in his pockets. Such a state was unheard of for any gentleman. Was he beyond the ordinary absent-minded? Certainly he was a little strange in his manner. There was that sudden overflowing of excitement, that odd abruptness. But that was, after all, no more than an acceptable departure from the strict conventions. So how did it come about that he was so utterly penniless?

She puzzled over it and puzzled over it, but came to no conclusion.

Of course, it was clear that old Mr Partington was the one who held the purse-strings. But he could not surely have left a grown son – Richard Partington must be thirty years of age – with his pockets bare as if he was a little boy too young even for pocket-money. Surely he could not.

Yet what other explanation was there?

Well, next week, when she would meet Richard Partington's father, might provide the answer. And it was curious, too, that she had not met old Mr Partington already. If it was he who was to pay her salary, her mean and disgraceful salary, ought he not at least to have been present at the interview she had just attended? Perhaps he had duties at his works, but could he not have stepped across to the house for ten minutes only? It seemed odd. It was odd.

But no doubt time would answer the enigma. If she took the offered post.

And, despite every reason not to, that she would do.

Chapter Two

Miss Unwin met the holder of the purse-strings at her new place of employment just one week after her disconcerting interview there. As she had known she would do, she had written accepting the post at the exact ending of the twenty-four-hour period in which to make up her mind that she had insisted on. She took up her duties at the beginning of the next week, and at dinner that evening she met old Mr Partington.

Quite what she had expected she was unable, after encountering the reality, precisely to remember. Certainly she had been prepared for some oddity. The man who could, it seemed, allow his thirty-year-old son to have not a penny in his pockets, the man who had offered so uncompromisingly a salary which many a cook would have scorned as wages, must be unusual. But the reality so far exceeded what she had contrived to imagine that the earlier picture was driven entirely from her mind.

She had come down from the room she had been given at the top of the house, a cheerless and unheated chamber, to the dining room which Richard Partington had already pointed out to her.

The moment that, a little cautiously, she opened the tall unpolished, dust-grimed door she saw the owner of the house standing in front of a once-magnificent marble fireplace, in which a tiny fire smoked and sulked, in all his strikingness of appearance.

He was very small, almost it seemed to her at that moment of shock a dwarf, though later she realised he was in fact no freak but simply as short as a man could be. In view of Richard Partington's own small stature she might have expected his father to be not much above five feet in height. But somehow, perhaps because his frame was not only short but slight as well, old Mr Partington looked very much smaller than his son.

If that had been all that was out of the ordinary in his appearance, she might have quickly got used to it. Yet she did not. In all the time she knew him – it was not very long – she never failed to feel an inner uncomfortableness on each occasion she was in the same room with him.

It was, she came to believe, because of the nature of his face, or rather of his whole head. Perched above that small, shrunken body, on which a suit of rusty black hung in lugubrious, time-polished folds, his head, which was almost entirely bald, seemed unnaturally large. Its size was emphasised by the thinness of the few hairs stretching across it and the pallid flesh seemed drawn tight as could be over skull, cheekbones and jaw. But nor was this all. From the enormous head there projected ears that were yet more out of proportion, pink-tinged flaps extended wide to catch the least sound, to examine it, to see what use could be made of it, to store it away.

'Father,' said Richard Partington as Miss Unwin, not without an inner stiffening of resolution, stepped into the room, 'this is our new governess, Miss Harriet Unwin. I – I have the greatest faith in her abilities.'

The little old man kept his eyes fastened on Miss Unwin. And she, with a strong effort of will, kept her gaze from dropping to the floor at her feet.

'Hm,' the old man said at last. 'I hardly see how she has had opportunity as yet to display any abilities – unless it is an ability to seize on the remuneration she has been offered.'

For a moment Miss Unwin, holding her eyes steadily on the small figure in front of the marble mantelpiece and its grudging fire, was tempted to reply that she had not so far seized on a single farthing of the little she was to receive. But she held herself in check.

'Good evening, sir,' she said instead. 'May I say how pleased I am to be under your roof, and to have charge of two girls as promising as your granddaughters.'

She contrived then to send out a quick look to Louisa and Maria, standing mutely in a far corner of the room.

'Promising? Promising?' their grandfather barked out. 'What do they promise but expense and yet more expense?'

There was no reply to be made to that, and Miss Unwin experienced the first of her many pangs of regret at having, so much against her better judgment, cast her lot in this strange place.

Nor was the smile, concealed by a quick turn of the head, which Richard Partington at once darted out to her much in the way of reassurance.

But, mercifully, the need to continue such an unpromising conversation was brought to an end by the sound of voices in the hall outside.

'Ah,' said Richard Partington, quickly seizing on the interruption, 'that will be our guests for the evening.'

'Yes,' his father chimed in, in a voice marked by no sign of hospitality, 'tonight we are entertaining, Miss Unwin. But I beg you to remember we are not people who frequently scatter what little we have under the eyes, and I may say the noses, of others.'

'Our guests,' Richard Partington broke in, making Miss Unwin think for a moment of a tired, flogged horse gallantly approaching yet once more a hedge it had found too high to jump before. 'Our guests are family relations and as such have a particular claim upon us.'

'Yes, that must be so,' Miss Unwin agreed, with as much force as she could muster.

But she let herself think, almost with bitterness, of her own foundling's life in which there could never be family relations to be offered, or not, hospitality.

11

'Distant cousins,' the small figure by the fireplace almost spat out.

'Yes, my Cousin Cornelia, Miss Cornelia Fulcher, and my Cousin John, her brother, Captain Fulcher, Jack as he likes to be called,' the gallant horse said. 'We made their acquaintance only a year or two ago. Cousin Cornelia's aunt on her father's side died and I chanced to see the notice in the newspaper and wrote.'

'Chanced. Chanced. Paid a halfpenny for the privilege of reading in a public ordinary the nonsense the newspapers print to catch their readers.'

'Less expensive, Father, than buying a newspaper,' Richard Partington murmured in reply.

Miss Unwin, who in her former place of employment had been accustomed to see as a matter of course two newspapers at the breakfast table every morning, felt a renewed sinking at the parsimony so casually put in front of her. Newspapers she preferred not to see herself if they could be avoided, but it seemed a gentleman's right to have them in the house. To learn that the father of her charges was reduced to hiring the sheets at a public dining room was yet another sign to her that she had made a bad decision in accepting the challenge of teaching the two stonily silent girls in the corner.

But she had little opportunity to muse. Before Richard Partington opened the tall, dusty mahogany door behind her there was time only for the little old man by the fire to dart out one single comment.

'Has ten thousand of her own in the Three Per Cents now. From the aunt.'

Then the heiress herself was in the room, her brother a pace behind her.

Miss Unwin's first thought was decidedly irreverent. *A good thing she has inherited her fortune, without it she would be hard pressed to find a husband*. And her second thought was yet more irreverent. *Even with it she will be pressed hard enough*.

Miss Cornelia Fulcher appeared to be in her late thirties, her very late thirties, and those years had taken their full toll. Both her face and figure were worn. Angularity was their most pronounced characteristic. And her nose, which was thin enough to remind Miss Unwin of a knife, was a raw red.

But thoughts such as those were to be kept to the very back of the mind, hardly to be thought at all. And perhaps Miss Fulcher's personal appearance would be no indication of her character.

Her brother seemed a good deal more prepossessing. To begin with he was reasonably tall, and after a period with two men of such limited stature as old Mr Partington and his son, it was somehow a relief to be in the same room as a person of normal height.

Yet even as this thought sprang irrepressibly to her mind, Miss Unwin felt a pang of guilt. Richard Partington had from their very first meeting been the soul of kindness. Even to think as slightly badly of him as she had, and for a fault he could not overcome, was a sort of betrayal.

Miss Unwin made up her mind that she would not by way of atonement allow herself at least for the next twenty-four hours one single reflection about how poorly she was being paid.

Besides, Captain Fulcher was not really in any way good looking. His face was too high coloured, a mottled red that spoke of the bottle, and his moustaches were surely too well curled, altogether too much proclaiming the military man.

'Very good of you, very good of you,' he said boomingly to old Mr Partington as he went up and offered his hand.

The little old man hesitated noticeably before extending his own hand, emerging like the head of a dried-up tortoise from his rusty black sleeve. But at last he did touch the Captain's fingers before rapidly withdrawing, as

13

if anxious not to lose any precious heat from his body. And, in view of the feebleness of the fire in the grate at his back, that was perhaps sensible.

The Captain, however, appeared not to notice the rebuff, though Miss Unwin was certain that a rebuff had been intended.

'Looking forward to a good dinner,' he said, his voice echoing round the high-ceilinged, inhospitable room. 'Had a wretched day. Every nag I put a guinea on came to a full stop in mid-career.'

'I cannot commiserate with you, sir,' old Mr Partington answered. 'A man who will risk his guineas, such guineas as he has, on the turn of speed shown by a horse deserves to lose every coin he possesses.'

Captain Fulcher took the remark as a joke.

'Gad,' he said, with a roar of laughter. 'Lose every coin he possesses. That's devilish near my position. Devilish near. If it wasn't for Cornelia . . . But that's another matter. 'Nother matter altogether. Now, sir, I've brought you some sherry. Small gift. Know you like it.'

From the pockets of his broadly cut, military-looking coat he produced a pair of bottles of sherry and, without anything in the way of permission, he proceeded to draw their corks with a corkscrew he seemed to know where to find on the sideboard. He then poured glasses for himself, old Mr Partington and, grudgingly a little, for Richard Partington.

Miss Unwin noted his behaviour as yet one more curious circumstance in this house of curious circumstances. But she had no time to think about it. Richard Partington had introduced her to Miss Fulcher.

'I am glad to hear those two little girls are to have better care,' she said in a near-whisper. 'When my brother and I were last here I could not help thinking that they needed more supervision. There was –'

She stopped and gave a great swallow so that the cords of her thin neck heaved.

14

She leant nearer Miss Unwin.

'There was dirt,' she hissed.

'I understand that until now they have been looked after entirely by Mr Partington's housekeeper,' Miss Unwin answered, tactfully as she could. 'And she must have many other duties.'

She wondered then herself just how many duties the housekeeper, a Mrs Meggs, of whom she had as yet only heard, did have. She suspected they were many indeed. So far she had seen no other servant. The door had been opened to her ring at the bell by Richard Partington himself, who had begun some explanation and had then abandoned it. He had told the cab-man, too, to put down her luggage in the hall, and there, but for a small valise she had herself taken to her room, it had remained. She had seen it as she had come down to dine.

'Yes, I suppose the good Mrs Meggs does do more than falls to the customary duties of a housekeeper,' Miss Fulcher said. 'Or so it seemed to me on our previous visits.'

She drew in a breath in something between a shudder and a sigh.

'I am a country dweller, Miss Unwin,' she went on. 'And, to tell you the truth, I am not surprised that the girls, living in London, should not be as clean as I should like. London is not a place where a lady can live with any true comfort.'

Miss Unwin was rather at a loss for a reply. Many ladies certainly lived in London without any feeling of discomfort, rather the opposite. But this was hardly a rejoinder she could make to her new employer's guest. She contented herself with a half-smile.

But a half-smile seemed to be all that was required.

Miss Fulcher again advanced her thin red nose till it was almost within an inch of Miss Unwin's.

'Flies,' she whispered. 'Flies. Horrible.'

Miss Unwin, from her days at a house in the country,

15

recalled not a few flies. Again a half-smile seemed to be her only recourse.

Luckily, at that moment the dining-room door was thrust open and a large tray, held in a pair of scrawny, almost gypsy-brown hands, appeared. It came to a momentary halt and then advanced once more, pushed forward by an elderly woman, old beyond any guessing of her age. Miss Unwin supposed that this must be Mrs Meggs. She was not an attractive person. Her face was as darkly brown as her hands and from a jutting chin there curled upwards a single bristle-thick white hair. A pair of sharp eyes looked rapidly round the room from beneath eyebrows composed of a tangle of more thick white hairs, and the bent attitude of her whole body only added to an impression of malevolent inquisitiveness.

On the extended tray there were seven soup plates and a small tureen.

'To table, to table,' old Mr Partington cackled out as Mrs Meggs banged down a plate at each place. 'The soup has cost a pretty penny to heat, I'll be bound, and it will be ill to let it cool.'

Miss Unwin felt a new sense of amazement.

But no sooner had the old man pronounced the extraordinary words than he let out a sharp moan of agony and doubled up, his hands clutching at his stomach.

Richard Partington at once ran towards him.

'Father,' he said. 'Another attack. Are you all right? Water. Can I give you some water?'

Miss Unwin, who had seen that on the dining table there was a carafe of water, went to it and poured some into the first tumbler that came to hand. She hurried along the length of the room and held the glass ready for Richard Partington to take and let his father, who was slowly straightening from his stomach-cramped position, sip at it.

However, the attack, though fierce, was short lived. The old man very quickly began to recover, and within two minutes appeared to be as spry as he had been when Miss Unwin had first seen him.

'What are you all waiting for?' he said, in a voice that was not far from a snarl. 'I told you the soup will be spoilt.'

Miss Unwin, who was hungry, noted with dismay how little the old man had helped her to. But it was dismay that lasted only until she tasted the watery liquid.

What it had been made from she could not guess. Certainly water was the chief ingredient, together with some salt and the faintest tinge of meat. The whole tasted so unpleasant she was unable to finish even the little she had been given.

While the soup was before them there was some little stiff conversation between the Partingtons and their guests. Miss Unwin thought it best not to attempt to join in. A governess, although she was considered to be a lady and thus fit to sit at the family table should that be thought convenient, was nonetheless always a dependant. Silence for such a one was golden.

A dish of mutton with some potatoes followed the soup. Again old Mr Partington as he carved put the smallest of helpings on to the plates. So small were they indeed that Captain Fulcher broke out in protest.

'I say, my dear fellow, give a chap a little more, won't you? When a chap's been at the races all day he gets a devilish sharp appetite.'

His host gave him a long look.

'Meat costs money, my dear sir,' he replied at last. 'I tell you, we do not eat as well every day in this house.'

Miss Unwin once more felt a lurch of dismay. She was not eating well now, not at all. Food as poor as this had not been put before her since she had left, many years ago it seemed, the workhouse that had been her earliest home. Was she now going to have to endure years of such austerity? And winters in rooms as cold as her bedroom above?

But the meat was at least rather more easy to eat than

the soup had been to drink, and she devoured her portion and the black-marked potatoes that went with it with something approaching eagerness.

But her hunger was not allayed. Would there be something in the nature of a pudding? Surely with guests at the table there must be.

She was not, however, to learn how far Mr Partington's unwilling hospitality stretched.

Before the shrunken old man had finished his own mutton – and Miss Unwin had observed that at least he had carved for himself no more than he had been willing to carve for others – his head suddenly jerked forward and struck the surface of the table in front of him, sending his plate with its few remains of hoarded meat skittering to the side.

Once more that moan of pain escaped his lips.

Richard Partington jumped from his chair.

'Father,' he said, 'this cannot go on. You are ill. Seriously ill. You must call the doctor.'

Slowly the old man forced his body into a half-upright position.

'Ill?' he ground out. 'I am not ill and well you know it. I am being poisoned. Poisoned. And no doctor is going to find a medicine that will put an end to that.'

Chapter Three

It seemed to Miss Unwin, looking back at the start of her life in the shabby house next to the pin factory, that the first evening she spent there had within it the whole pattern of her existence afterwards. The bone-chilling cold, the grim sparseness of the meals, the embittered meanness of old Mr Partington with the half-hidden sweet apologetic smiles of his son, and, running through it all, the old man's sharp bouts of painful illness.

Another note that varied as little was his adamant refusal to have the doctor called. True, he did not repeat, at least in Miss Unwin's hearing, the claim that he was being poisoned, and she came at that period to believe the words he had gasped out at the dinner table on her first evening under his roof were no more than so much unthinking fury, though later she was to recall them vividly enough.

But in the days and weeks that followed that first appalling, unforgettable meal the memory of that particular moment slipped into oblivion. Other meals, even less appetising, even more parsimonious, put that first one into the shade.

On all occasions when there were no visitors, and the Fulchers were the only ones ever to cross the threshold of the cold, uncared for house, only one course was served at dinner. It was almost always the same, largely potatoes, generally some other vegetable – whatever was cheapest in the market, Miss Unwin soon decided – and with those a little meat, which usually Mrs Meggs served to old Mr Partington alone.

This had happened at the second dinner Miss Unwin ate in the house.

Mrs Meggs came into the dining room with her tray on which there were two dishes, one containing a fair quantity of boiled potatoes, though already Miss Unwin could see that they were more black than white, and the other with a lesser quantity of dark coarse cabbage. But in addition there was one plate on which there lay some meat. Miss Unwin, hungry after a small breakfast and as small a lunch, could not refrain from looking with more closeness than was properly polite at what they were to get. She was unable to decide whether the dark and stringy pieces on this solitary plate were mutton or beef. But soon she found the question was not one which would concern her. The plate was put fairly and squarely in front of the master of the house, and before Richard Partington, herself and the two girls, empty plates were banged down by Mrs Meggs, as if challengingly.

It was a challenge which, to Miss Unwin's considerable embarrassment, Richard Partington at once took up.

'Mrs Meggs,' he said, staring hard at a point on the ceiling above him, 'is there no meat for Miss Unwin?'

'There's not,' Mrs Meggs answered, plonking down the two dishes of vegetables for him to serve himself from.

Richard Partington's round open face went red with immediate anger.

'Father,' he said, looking along the table to the old man, 'for myself I do not mind, but I feel that it is our duty towards one who has come to live under our roof that we provide her with the common necessities of life.'

'Common necessities, sir? Potatoes and cabbage are those. She can eat them, or go. I did not want a governess for your children.'

For a long moment Richard Partington held his peace. Miss Unwin, watching him covertly as she kept her eyes down to the empty plate in front of her, realised however that further words were not far from his lips. She wished passionately that he would keep silent. But she doubted whether he would remain so for long.

Her doubts were soon resolved.

'Father,' Richard Partington said, grating the word out, 'Father, how does it come about then that you have meat in front of you?'

'That is my business, sir.'

'No, Father, while a lady brought into this house to care for my daughters is without meat to eat and while you have it, it is my business as much as yours.'

Now it was the turn of the old man to be silent.

Miss Unwin sat still, looking unswervingly at her empty plate. Richard Partington sat glaring at his father, the two dishes of steaming vegetables growing cold in front of him. Louisa and Maria shifted to and fro on their chairs. Miss Unwin guessed that they were as hungry as herself and as eager for the dispute to end so that the food, little appetising as it was, could come to them.

At last the old man at the head of the table made a grudging reply.

'Mrs Meggs puts meat in front of me, as you well know, sir, because I am not at present in good health. She believes I need the nourishment so that I can work to keep you all in the idleness you prefer. And that is all that is to be said on this subject.'

Miss Unwin wondered whether this was true. Would her knight errant, little though she wished it, spring again to her defence?

But, evidently, the challenge he had issued before had been as far as he felt able to assert himself against the formidable character of his father.

'I may speak of this again when the time is more appropriate,' he said.

But he spoke the words so quietly that Miss Unwin had more guessed what they were than heard them, and she doubted whether the old man at the other end of the table, for all the extraordinary size of the two ears that jutted

21

from his bald white skull, had caught more than a rebellious murmur.

And that he had felt able to ignore.

So in the days that followed it was potatoes and other vegetables that Miss Unwin ate. Only very occasionally at times when Cousin Cornelia and her brother were not visitors did some meat get served, and when it did she half regretted it so nearly tainted did it taste.

One day Richard Partington began an attempt, she realised, to explain matters.

'I am afraid I do not see as much of my girls as I should like, Miss Unwin.'

'No, sir. They would benefit from a father's attention, when they have had no mother to care for them.'

Richard Partington heaved a deep sigh.

'I wish it could be otherwise. I wish —'

He broke off.

Then there flashed out that rueful, engaging sideways smile.

'Oh, Miss Unwin, it's useless to attempt to conceal from you the true state of affairs. You must have seen what my situation is from your very first day in this house.'

'I do not wish to know more than it is proper for me to know, sir.'

'Sir? Sir? No, please, Miss Unwin, do not call me by such a title. I need a friend. Sometimes I think I need a friend more than ever man did.'

Miss Unwin felt herself at a loss, and contrived to say nothing in answer.

Certainly in the time she had been in the house she had already come to feel for Richard Partington a great deal of sympathy. He was a pleasant person. She detected in him, of necessity deep buried, the springs of generosity. She would not find it difficult to share friendship with him.

But from the first moment she had contemplated becoming a governess she had known she must hold to one inflexible rule. If ever anywhere she found herself under the same roof as a gentleman whose affections were not engaged, she would keep herself strictly aloof. From all that she had heard she knew that to do otherwise was to court disaster.

She had heard too much of young governesses seduced by the sons of the houses where they taught. That led easily and swiftly to ruin. It led, she knew, to the streets. Equally she had heard of cases where honourable love had been offered by a susceptible gentleman to a governess with some pretensions to beauty, and of the almost invariable opposition the hint of such a misalliance created in the young man's family. That opposition could bring ruin almost as final as a life on the streets.

Yet here, in the cold, cold house next to the pin factory, she felt her situation was in some way different.

For one thing she had learnt that the reason Miss Cornelia Fulcher, that hater of the flies and dirt of London, had visited the capital was that a marriage between herself and her cousin was contemplated. So presumably Richard Partington's affections were already fixed.

His father spoke of the match on occasion in unmistakable terms.

'Well, Richard,' Miss Unwin had heard him say, 'the life of a country gentleman should suit you well. You have a great capacity for ease.'

And Richard Partington had remained silent, seemingly in agreement.

Equally, Miss Fulcher made it plain on her every visit that it was Richard she had come to see.

'Oh, Cousin Richard, I cannot agree with you more. You put it so well, so well.'

And really, Miss Unwin had thought, Richard Partington had said nothing then that was not a mere ordinary observation.

'Oh, Richard, I so look forward to the day I need come no more to London. The noise of town, its dirt and

23

those wretched, wretched flies everywhere.'

'Come, Cornelia, there are surely no more flies in London than near a farmyard in the country.'

'That may be so, Richard, my dear, but I assure you there is no farmyard within half a mile of Stavely.'

'Is there not? I thought when I visited you on the sad occasion of your aunt's funeral that I observed a farm within a hundred yards of the house gates.'

'No, that is nothing. One could not call it a farm. There is a man there who keeps a few cows, no more.'

'And those cows attract not a single fly?'

'Now, Richard, you tease. You must know in truth that London abounds with the filthy creatures. Why, in Jack's lodgings I have had to have fly-papers hung in every room. They are an abomination, but what else is to be done?'

Here old Mr Partington had abruptly intervened.

'Nothing is to be done, madam. Let a few flies have their little day. The fly-paper men are rogues, to the last one of them. I cannot tell you what they attempt to make one pay.'

'And that, sir,' Cousin Cornelia replied, with a trilling little laugh, 'must be because you make no attempt to pay them.'

Old Mr Partington had looked for a moment then as if he would produce a reply that would send this distant cousin scuttling from the house. But he had controlled himself, and Miss Unwin thought she knew why. If his son were to marry the lady with ten thousand in the Three Per Cents of her own, he himself would no longer have to support son, nor son's daughters, nor the governess they needed.

And to this sentiment Richard Partington apparently agreed. So, if he wanted friendship as he claimed he did, it would be a friendship free of any question of anything more. She should not hesitate in agreeing to it. Yet she did. She hardly knew why.

24

But in the matter of Richard Partington's daughters needing a governess, Miss Unwin had very soon found this to be decidedly the case. The fact was that since their mother had died in giving them birth they had been brought up entirely by the ancient Mrs Meggs, and Mrs Meggs was less fitted to bring up children than she was to be a housekeeper, a task in which her chief efforts seemed to be directed to achieving as little expenditure as she possibly could.

So Louisa and Maria had learnt almost nothing. They could barely read, Miss Unwin discovered on the first shivering morning that she had tried to teach them in an unheated room at the top of the house that had been set aside as a schoolroom. They had learnt few manners, and few habits of cleanliness. Miss Fulcher had indeed been correct about the latter, though it had been a very easy matter to put right.

Their father, in the little his duties at the pin works had allowed him to see of them, had attempted to do what he could. Their grandfather had never regarded them, it seemed, as other than an extra expense. And Mrs Meggs, bent and malevolent, had no manners or cleanliness of her own to impart.

Bit by bit in her first weeks in the house Miss Unwin had begun to improve the situation. At least, she found, both girls were usually willing.

'Oh, Miss Unwin, read us a story, you are so clever,' Louisa might cry out.

'But you should read a story for yourselves. Louisa, you read the first page, and Maria the next.'

'We will try, Miss Unwin,' Maria sagely answered. 'But it is so difficult.'

Here she was speaking the truth.

But one of Miss Unwin's earliest discoveries had been that her pupils both very readily told lies. She hardly blamed them. Almost no effort had been made with them to inculcate the virtues of truth, and she knew from her

25

own workhouse childhood that lies come readily to lips that need them to escape punishment or rebuke, just or unjust.

Sometimes, too, it was difficult to tell whether the girls were lying or not.

'Miss Unwin, you know Grandpapa is very, very rich.'

Miss Unwin, still hungry after a meagre lunch of dry bread and a little hard cheese, promptly suspected Louisa of starting some tarradiddle with an as yet unexplained object.

'I know no such thing, Louisa.'

'Oh, but Miss Unwin, that is true,' Maria said, as much as to imply that many other things her sister might announce were not so true.

'Yes, yes, Miss Unwin,' Louisa broke in in her own defence. 'Grandpapa has heaps of gold. We've seen it.'

'Then I'm sure you should not have done.'

'No, we know we shouldn't, Miss Unwin,' said Louisa quite cheerfully.

'Yes,' said Maria. 'He hides it all so carefully, but before you came and we started to have lessons there was never anything to do, so we used to go exploring.'

'And that,' Louisa triumphantly finished, 'is when we found out. Do you want to know where he hides it all, Miss?'

'I most certainly do not. And nor do I think you can be right.'

'But we are, we are.'

This was a chorus of two.

'No, I suppose you must have seen something that you thought was gold, or seen some gold your grandfather had in the house one day to buy materials that were needed at the works. So what you two must do is to forget all about it. Yes?'

'Yes, Miss.'

It had not taken Miss Unwin more than a few days to

make the girls see that when she said a thing was to be done it was to be done.

But it was to take a good deal longer before she had instilled into the pair of them, and particularly into Louisa, the notion that they had to behave well even when she was not present, that they had to obey commands that had not been directly given.

As before long she was to discover, with consequences more than she had reckoned on.

But in the meanwhile the pattern of her life, the common task, the daily round, went on. It was enlivened only by the visits of Cousin Cornelia and her brother, and often these were little enough enlivening.

Once, however, Captain Fulcher's presence did bring a spurt of activity out of the common, something Miss Unwin was to find disagreeable rather than otherwise.

'Good evening, sir, good evening,' Captain Fulcher had boomily greeted Mr Partington in the dining room, to which as usual he and his sister had been ushered by the ancient, hair-sprouting Mrs Meggs. There was never a fire lit in any other room of the house in the evenings and in consequence nowhere else to entertain guests. If Cousin Cornelia and Captain Fulcher arrived even as much as an hour before dinner was ready, in the dining room they stood or sat.

'Allow me to present you with a small gift.'

The Captain then produced, as he always did, a pair of bottles of sherry. Miss Unwin suspected he brought the gift to ensure that he himself had something to drink, a suspicion reinforced by the speed with which the Captain went to the sideboard, found the corkscrew and began removing the corks from the bottles.

Miss Unwin saw the old man's eyes glisten. Though he resolutely refused ever to have even ale in the house and constantly praised 'good clean water' she knew that in fact he relished a glass of wine.

Captain Fulcher knew it too.

'Come, sir, let's drink. I've had a day that beggars belief. Damn near beggared me, come to that.'

The Captain never heeded the presence of his sister, let alone that of Miss Unwin, in the matter of guarding his language.

Mr Partington gave him a sharply contemptuous look.

'You have been to some racecourse then?' he asked.

'Where else is there to go?' Captain Fulcher answered. 'Damn it, there's no one at the club for play till late in the evening, and a fellow can't just sit and read the damned newspaper all day.'

'No, sir, he cannot. Richard will tell you that. We have no newspaper in this house. I'll not have him linger at the breakfast table when he could be earning his bread next door.'

Captain Fulcher sighed.

'I suppose some fellows must work,' he said. 'But I was brought up to believe that the Army and the Church were the only professions fit for gentlemen. And you can't see me a clergyman, I should hope.'

'No, Cousin,' Richard Partington broke in then, his face redder by the minute. 'I cannot see you in such an honourable occupation.'

But Captain Fulcher, busy pouring the sherry, failed to note the anger his cousin had showed.

Miss Unwin noted it and sympathised with the feelings it betrayed.

She saw, too, that Miss Fulcher, though she could not but have heard her brother's loud remark and Richard Partington's sharp reply, seemingly failed to understand the careless insult that had been offered and the offence it had caused.

But there was nothing Miss Unwin could do to indicate to her employer, as she felt the twins' father to be, that he had at least one hearer who felt for him. Dully she watched Captain Fulcher pull out the second bottle's cork with a great flourish and pour from it wine for himself and Richard.

But her discomfort had not long to be endured. Out in the hall there came the sudden sound of a man's raised voice.

Miss Unwin realised then that she had, in fact, heard the door bell, and it was only because of Captain Fulcher's behaviour that she had not asked herself who could be calling at the house at such an hour.

Her query was not long in finding an answer.

Mrs Meggs opened the dining-room door by a few inches and thrust in her deep-brown face.

'There's a man wants to see the Captain,' she said.

'To see me? Who the devil –'

But Mrs Meggs was at that moment thrust aside, almost bodily, and a dark stranger came walking into the room, a man heavy with plumpness like an overripe fruit.

'Mr Davis,' the Captain exclaimed.

'Yes, Captain,' the newcomer answered, smiling without humour. 'We had an appointment at my office, but I believe you must have let it slip your mind.'

Captain Fulcher seemed, for once, thoroughly disconcerted.

'I – I would have come,' he spluttered. 'You know there's no question of my not – That is, damn it, man, this is hardly the time to conduct business. Or the place. No, damn it, not the place at all.'

'Well, Captain, the place is not of my choosing,' the heavily plump Mr Davis responded. 'The place I chose was my own office, and the time was an hour since.'

'Well, I dare say, I dare say,' Captain Fulcher answered, beginning to recover his sangfroid. 'And it did escape my mind. But why the devil you could not have waited I cannot tell.'

'I have waited, Captain. The bills are overdue by a week and more.'

Then Miss Unwin finally understood. Mr Davis was a moneylender, and no doubt Captain Fulcher had avoided paying his debts to him out of more than mere forgetfulness. So the newcomer had tracked him down and was intending to shame him in front of friends.

But old Mr Partington was not a person to be embarrassed when any matter of money was in question.

He came forward now, a small but by no means unimpressive figure, his over-large head projecting in front of his body and the two great ears on either side of his fleshless skull seemingly poised to detect the slightest trick of meaning in anything the intruder might have to say.

'So you are a usurer,' the old man spat out.

'It is an occupation, a necessary occupation,' Mr Davis answered, already on the defensive.

'An occupation fit for none but the vilest wretches in society,' Mr Partington snapped back. 'Leave my house this instant, sir, or I'll have you thrown out on your neck.'

Miss Unwin thought, with a sudden spurt of inner amusement, of old Mrs Meggs attempting to throw out the plump moneylender. But Mr Davis was unaware that the ancient housekeeper was the only servant under their roof and was evidently prepared to treat Mr Partington's threat with respect.

'There is no need for violence,' he said. 'No need whatsoever. I am a peaceable man. I want only to attend to my business and let others attend to theirs.'

'Then attend to your business in your own premises,' Captain Fulcher, emboldened by old Mr Partington's contemptuous treatment of the moneylender, broke in.

'I'm going, I'm going. But you'll come tomorrow, Captain? The bills are seven days overdue.'

'I'll come if I've time,' Captain Fulcher replied with a great show of languid uninterest.

And with that unlikely reassurance Mr Davis found his own way out.

'Deuced awkward,' said the Captain when he heard the front door close with a heavy thud.

He turned to his host.

'I suppose you wouldn't . . .' he began.

Then he saw the cold look in the little old man's eyes and his voice faltered to a stop.

No, thought Miss Unwin, if you had hoped for money to pay off those bills from that source you were more hopeful than any foolish man has a right to be. And she wondered why Captain Fulcher should have even thought that the owner of this dismal, cold, inhospitable house would possess wealth which he could borrow to pay off those racing debts of his.

That was a mystery to which she was to begin to have the key that very night, and in a most unexpected way.

As soon as the meal was over, as was her custom she took the twins up to bed and then retired to her own room. She felt it her duty not to burden her employers with her presence, although she little relished the never-relieved cold of her chamber.

As usual she undressed rapidly, felt grateful that she had at least a thick flannel nightgown and slipped between the cold harsh sheets.

She lay and shivered. Within a few minutes, she knew, she would be a little warmer and then she would venture to put her arms out from beneath the covers and by the wavering light of her tallow candle – something which Mrs Meggs doled out only with many a comment on how quickly they were used – she would read for as long as she could bear to. The studies which she was undertaking to better her position in life were slipping, she knew, far behind in the course she had set for herself. But endurance went only so far. The attainment of the high standard she hoped to reach, a standard that might one day enable her to open a small school of her own, would be delayed by some months. It would be delayed even

31

longer, however, were she to catch a chill or perhaps the rheumatic fever.

So, still shivering, she poked her arms out of bed and took up Mrs Mackintosh's *Principles of Domestic Science*.

But she had hardly read a page of the book's uncompromising prose when a faint noise disturbed her. She stopped reading and listened.

The noise was repeated. A scuffle and bump.

What was it? There should be no such sounds at the top of the house. Mrs Meggs had her bed somewhere in the kitchen where she was doubtless a good deal warmer for the presence of the stove, its scanty coals still glowing. Was it then some intruder?

Miss Unwin lay, still listening.

An intruder was surely altogether unlikely in this barred and barred again house. Had the sound perhaps been the twins? They had always slept soundly up till now, and when she had left them had both certainly seemed to be already asleep.

But perhaps one had woken for some reason.

Miss Unwin slipped out of bed, pushed her feet into her felt slippers, pulled her wrap round her shoulders and cautiously opened her door. She saw no one. But by the flickering light of her candle she noticed that the door of the girls' room was an inch or so ajar.

She crossed over and peered in. Two empty beds. What could the pair of them be doing?

Swiftly she went down the stairs, her feet making no sound in their soft slippers.

No sign of the children on the floor below. She went down the next flight.

What if Captain Fulcher and his sister were suddenly to emerge from the dining room? She was by no means fit to be seen, with only her wrap to hide her nightdress. But the twins were plainly doing something they should not be and they must be stopped.

But neither of them was to be seen on the ground floor.

Had they gone down to the basement? They must have done. But what could they have in mind? Visiting the larder to see if there was anything to eat there? Their dinner had been meagre enough, and perhaps they had reckoned that by now Mrs Meggs would be safely asleep. She hardly blamed the girls if this was their object, though she must not let them see that when she caught them.

She hurried on down the stone steps leading to the basement, blowing out her candle and taking more care now not to be heard. If the children were to be caught it was better to catch them fully in the act.

But when she did come across the twins, bending over something on the stone-flagged floor near the door to the back of the house, two thin white shapes in their bed-gowns, a guttering stub of candle illuminating them, she experienced a shock of utter surprise.

The children had managed to lever up a flagstone, apparently much thinner than its fellows, and had revealed a shallow sunken pit. And in the pit there gleamed pile upon pile of golden sovereigns.

Chapter Four

For several long moments Miss Unwin, the cold of the basement flagstones striking her feet through the felt of her slippers, stood staring between the twins' thin curved backs at the pit of glowing gold revealed by their candle stub.

So the girls had not been inventing when they had told her that their grandfather had heaps of gold and that they knew where it was. So in this chill and miserable house there was the wherewithal to lead lives of decent comfort, of luxury even.

But she could not go on standing there looking, and thinking.

'Girls,' she said sharply.

Louisa screamed. Maria gasped.

'Well, what are you doing down here at this hour of the night?'

Neither replied.

'Well?'

'Please, Miss Unwin,' the quieter Maria said at last. 'Please, we didn't mean any harm.'

'Then why did you come creeping down here?'

Louisa scrambled to her feet and gave her a mutinous glare.

'We were hungry,' she said.

'Hungry, indeed? And were you going to eat your grandfather's coins?'

'No, Miss,' Maria said. 'But we were going to take one, only one.'

'To take one is almost as bad as taking a hundred. You

know they are not yours. You know that it is wrong to steal.'

'But we were hungry, Miss,' Louisa broke in. 'I don't mean just hungry tonight, though we were, but we're hungry almost all the time.'

'So what we were going to do,' added Maria, 'was to take just one of Grandpapa's sovereigns, and then, as we go out for walks now that you've come to look after us, Miss, we were going to go into a sweetshop and buy some nice things.'

It was then, just before Miss Unwin was going to utter a second stern rebuke and to mention punishment, that Louisa added some words that kept her silent.

'We've never been to a sweetshop, Miss.'

Miss Unwin's heart melted. Her own earliest days had had no sweetshops in them. Indeed, one of her most vivid memories was of a little rich boy in a passing carriage throwing out a 'gobstopper', a big ball of layered sugars each in a different colour, and how she had rushed at it, picked it up all dust-covered from the road and had thrust it instantly into her mouth. In her mind now she tasted again the tongue-drying dust that had so quickly yielded to the unimagined delight of the sweet, sweet sugar.

But evidently Louisa and Maria had been deprived for all their lives of any such joy, and it was a joy that they were entitled to. It was a joy they were entitled to by those very piles of softly glowing sovereigns lying there under their eyes at this moment.

'Put back that stone,' she said with sharpness. 'And if I ever suspect either of you of coming here again there will be the severest punishment. You understand?'

'Yes, Miss.'

'Yes, Miss Unwin.'

Two voices in hushed obedience, conscious of a note that they had not hitherto heard from her, a note of anger. Hastily between them the two slid and scraped the thin flagstone back into place again.

'And now to bed with you both, at once.'

The scuttle of bare feet on the stone steps and two whiteclad figures disappearing, leaving their stub of candle guttering weirdly behind them. And Miss Unwin.

A Miss Unwin who was very thoughtful indeed.

The girls' discovery, she realised, put her in a very difficult situation. It must be her duty to tell the guardian of this hidden gold that his secret had been discovered. She owed him that, beyond doubt. But she owed something, too, to Maria and Louisa, cruelly deprived as she now doubly knew them to be. Nor did she look forward to telling old Mr Partington what she nevertheless knew that she must. For someone who had hoarded all that wealth away to learn that its hiding-place was known might be an almost mortal blow. The giver of that blow was likely to receive a hard return, and the two innocents who had first made the discovery were likely to pay dear for it as well.

Yet next day, as soon as she had the least opportunity, she went to see the hoarder of those golden yellow sovereigns. She had decided before she fell asleep between the once-again cold sheets of her bed the night before that there would be no chance of finding old Mr Partington alone in the house itself. He was accustomed not to return in the evening from the pin works till shortly before the dinner hour. Once back, he spent the time in the dining room where there was a fire, the one which after that first day in the bitterly cold schoolroom she herself had insisted on having in the little parlour for the girls' lessons having been scrupulously raked out by Mrs Meggs as soon as the lessons were over.

After their scanty dinner Mr Partington always sat on with his son in the dining room until the hour for tea. Then, once he had swallowed his extra large cup of Mrs Meggs's extraordinarily weak brew, he went up to bed. In the mornings there was breakfast hurriedly eaten in the chill dining room and promptly afterwards out he would

37

go to immure himself in the works.

But Miss Unwin had gathered from Richard Partington that at the works his father spent all day in his own room. Richard himself, he had told her with that rueful smile of his, had a desk just outside its door with a high stool not very different from those of the clerks nearby busy copying letters and bills and keeping the ledgers up to date.

So, if old Mr Partington was to be bearded at all, in his room at the pin works it would have to be.

Miss Unwin gave him precisely one hour after the start of his day to read the letters that had come in by the post and to dictate his answers. Then she set off in her turn having given strict instructions to Louisa and Maria about the column in Butter's *Spelling* that they were to get by heart in her absence.

She hoped that absence would not be long.

All she envisaged was going to the works, sending in to Mr Partington to say she had something serious to inform him of, making her confession and leaving at once. And she thought of what she would have to say as, somehow, a confession. Her own confession. Not a confession made by her on the part of Mr Partington's granddaughters. She knew that the old man would feel it was deeply wrong of her, a stranger, to have learnt his secret. However much care she might take in the telling to make it clear that she had been in no way to blame for knowing that secret, the old miser would hate her for her knowledge.

Because his secret was, she realised with new force, a terribly shameful one.

Yet let him understand that she knew of it she must. It was her plain duty, whatever wrath it brought down on her head.

But, crossing the cobbled yard that separated the house from the works, it was all she could do to force herself to put one foot in front of the other.

She entered the tall red-brick factory through a narrow

38

door of heavy wood which opened with a groan as she gave it a tentative push. Inside, her ears were at once assaulted by the frenzied clatter of iron upon iron. In front of her, extending over the whole ground floor of the building, were the machines that pressed and twisted and forced together the little pins which had made Mr Partington his great fortune. His great fortune that, Miss Unwin now knew, must have almost all been converted into golden sovereigns and buried in the pit beneath the thin flagstone in the basement of the house. Buried there or, she suspected, in various other places in the house as well.

She was about to approach one of the operatives, head bent over his machine, ceaselessly watching its clattering cranks and moving wheels and from time to time pulling one of its long wooden-handled levers, when she noticed a flight of open wooden stairs leading to a large platform at first-floor level. Looking up, she saw that on the platform there were the ranged desks of the clerks, with other studiously bent heads at work.

She climbed up.

At the top, the clerk whose desk was nearest the stairs looked up from his laborious copying as her shadow fell across his page.

'Can I help you, madam?' he asked.

'Yes, my name is Miss Unwin and I have come to see Mr Partington on a most urgent matter,' she answered, feeling that unless she stated with as much force as she could that her business was pressing she would not be allowed to hinder the pin-works owner's steady acquisition of yet more and more gold sovereigns to add to his hoard.

'I will see if he is disengaged,' the clerk said.

Miss Unwin inclined her head in acknowledgement.

The man went over to a partitioned-off part of the high, busy platform. Presumably behind it sat old Mr Partington.

Miss Unwin noticed then, with a certain relief, that Richard Partington's somewhat larger high desk just outside the door of his father's room was unoccupied. No doubt it was Richard's duty sometimes to go about here and there seeing to business for the firm. She had not liked the idea of having to visit his father without telling him why she was entering the sanctum. But, had he questioned her or even raised an interrogative eyebrow, she would have been duty-bound to keep from him this secret of his father's.

Just as she was duty-bound now, in one moment, more, to tell the aged miser that she knew it.

'The Master will see you,' the clerk said, returning.

Miss Unwin realised from the very way the clerk declined to look her full in the face that the old man inside had expressed, doubtless in highly vigorous terms, anger at anyone daring to break in on his business day. But he had said that he would see her. Curiosity, she knew, was a powerful force and she had counted on it.

She walked through the ranks of clerks' desks. Not a head was lifted from the work in front of them. But one by one the scratching pens slowed in their tasks.

She knocked at the closed door of Mr Partington's room.

'Come in,' she heard the old man bark drily.

She turned the wooden doorknob, pushed open the door and entered.

Her employer was sitting behind a dusty leather-topped desk, evidently on a chair specially raised higher than usual from the ground since his smallness of stature was no longer apparent. But the size of his large head was even more evident than usual. And the two extra large ears projecting from its fleshlessness seemed prepared more than ever to sift out the last shade of meaning, the least hesitation, in what she might have to say.

'Well?'

There was no help for it now. No beating about the bush

would be possible. Not the quickest exchange of preliminary civilities.

She took a breath.

'Mr Partington,' she said, 'I have to tell you that your granddaughters have discovered –'

She faltered then. But faltered only for an instant.

'Have discovered what it is that lies beneath the flagstone near the basement door in the house.'

It was said. It was done. The words had been spoken. The knowledge that the old miser's secret was a secret no more had been revealed.

Miss Unwin waited for the thunderbolt to descend.

Her words were received in silence.

She brought herself at last to lift up her gaze, which as she had spoken the unsayable thing she had not been able to raise higher than the paper-strewn surface of the desk in front of the old man. She looked now full and fair at the large white-domed head.

It seemed as if it had been in an instant turned to true stone. The eyelids above the cold eyes did not so much as blink. The lips, pale almost as the skin surrounding them, did not quiver. It was hard to detect any breath issuing from the tense nostrils.

Then, at last, there was a movement, a little forward jerk of that over-large head.

Miss Unwin was positively relieved to find that she had not in truth struck her employer dead.

'Gold.'

The word now came out from between the hardly parted lips. It was only the one short syllable. But in it there was a world of desolation.

Miss Unwin began a rapid jabber of explanation, telling once again how she had heard mysterious noises in the house as she had lain in bed the night before, how she had tracked them down, what she had seen, what the twins had said by way of explanation.

And all the while, as she poured out the history which

41

she had gone over and over in her mind till she knew it as well as she knew the list of the names of the Kings and Queens of England, she was thinking.

What had made him do it? How could he over years and years have stored away coin after coin in that way? How could he have deprived his two little grandchildren of all that they might have had, even down to their never having so much as visited a sweetshop? How could he have deprived his own son of even the trifling amount of a cab fare so that he had been overcome with embarrassment in front of a prospective governess? How could he have deprived himself of food, warmth, clothes?

As she came towards the end of her recital she saw that into the old man's eyes there was creeping again his look of habitual cunning. She welcomed it even. It was better far than the look of stony death that had greeted her first words.

When at last she had come to a breathless end the miser spoke.

'It is all that I have,' he said, glancing up at her with patent slyness. 'Those few sovereigns stored away there. All that I have. It is best to keep them there in that fashion, you know. Banks are never to be trusted. Servants peep and peer into anybody's bank book.'

Miss Unwin thought of the 'servants' in the house on the other side of the cobbled yard. Old Mrs Meggs, hardly able to read. Herself, perhaps. Though of course she was not a servant, the old man very likely considered her such. But she had been in the house only a few weeks, while that deep little pit of hidden sovereigns must have taken years to amass. Besides those in the other hiding-places elsewhere in the house which she was sure existed.

The thought of them must have manifested itself somehow in her expression. And the consumedly avaricious man looking up at her had at once seen that she had penetrated his next secret.

'You know where they are?' he barked out. 'You have

poked and pried till you have found the others?'

'No, sir. No. I would scorn to do anything of the sort. I have told you by what accident I came upon that one hiding-place. I have done nothing to seek out any more.'

Suddenly the little old man pushed himself to his feet, tumbling down from his high chair. His white skull of a face darkened to red anger such as Miss Unwin had not seen in all the time she had been in his house.

'You lie!' he screamed. 'You lie. You lie.'

Then, as if even through his wild swirl of rage some old remnant of the caution with which up till now he had kept his fearful secret had returned, he dropped his voice to a fierce hoarse whisper and thrust himself forward nearer to her.

A wave of nauseating breath spumed out at her, and she saw, unpleasantly close, the line of yellow irregular teeth, all loose in the oddly blue-looking gums.

She stepped back a pace.

'Sir,' she said, 'I do not lie.'

She must have been able to convey in the words all the inner belief that they carried, because the old man slowly clambered back on to his chair.

'There is very little there, there where you saw them,' he said. 'There is much less than it appears. The pit is shallow, very shallow. There cannot be more than fifty pounds there. Not even so much.'

Miss Unwin thought of the neat piles of softly glowing coins she had seen. The recess beneath the flagstone might not be all that deep but she had no doubt that each pile of sovereigns in it must contain fifty coins itself. And there had been too many piles to count before she had ordered the twins to slide back the stone that covered them.

But the old miser, she knew, needed to believe that his secret had not been wholly penetrated.

'Yes, sir,' she answered. 'I am sure that the sum I believed I saw there may not be so very great. But

43

nevertheless I felt it my duty to tell you that the presence of even that much money in a place where it can be reached is known to your granddaughters. And to myself.'

The old man pushed his big hairless head forward half an inch.

'Known,' he said. 'Known. Known to you, and to those children. Children will talk. Will talk. Will prattle. Cannot be silenced.'

'Nevertheless, sir,' Miss Unwin broke in on his almost incoherent muttering. 'Nevertheless, I have spoken to the girls in a manner which I think they will not forget. I have told them that they should never have learnt what lies beneath that stone, that it is your particular secret for you to keep. I think they will not speak of it, to anyone, at any time.'

But even as she pronounced the words, which at the moment of utterance she believed to be entirely true, a thought rose up from some recess of her mind.

It presented itself as a picture. A curious picture. It showed two young girls, twins, dressed neatly but simply as she now saw to it that Louisa and Maria dressed, standing to either side of a person they should not have been associated with. The unmistakable roué, Captain Fulcher. Standing to either side of him, looking up laughingly, teasingly, and prattling away.

They had been doing, unusually for them, just what their grandfather had feared they might do at some future time, prattling and joking – and letting slip in all innocence something of the secret of his hoarded wealth.

Because there was a word that Miss Unwin heard in her mind to accompany this picture. There was innocent prattle in which the word 'Gold' had been said and repeated.

And the word had been said. Its speaking was not a fear for the future, but something done in the past and not to be undone. And it was, too, she thought, from the very way it had been mentioned an old often repeated joke of the twins with which they had teased the Captain.

The Captain had been embarrassed by the laughing attack made on him. It had been plain to Miss Unwin the one time she had witnessed it that he was not a person used to children. He had no knowledge of the way to talk to the young. Indeed, she had said to herself at the time, the sort of people Captain Fulcher knows how to talk to are low jockeys and stableboys, the hangers-on at the racecourses from whom he hopes to gather information that may win him the bets he almost always speaks of as having lost.

But nonetheless he must have heard what the twins had prattled to him about. Have heard more than once indeed giggling boasts that if he had lost money at the racecourse they knew where there were piles and piles of gold to make him happy again. No doubt he had paid scarcely any attention to the hornet-like buzzings of the two children. He had plainly been relieved on the occasion Miss Unwin remembered when she had told the girls that they must not annoy a visitor and had whisked them away.

But still that word 'gold' had been spoken in his presence. Was it possible that he had later wondered whether the twins' childish boasts concealed truth? Could he have asked them just where the gold they had laughingly spoken of was to be found? Or had he even made a point of listening at other times to the two of them talking together, have picked up some little hint passed from one to the other?

Did he, too, know Mr Partington's secret?

Was this the reason that he had thought it worthwhile to make his attempt, at once seen to be hopeless, to borrow from his aged cousin in order to pay off the moneylender, Mr Davis? Or, worse, far worse, was this the reason why no more had been heard of the plump Mr Davis? When the moneylender had burst in on them he had spoken of bills already a week overdue. But after that, so far as she herself knew, he had no longer been pressing. Was it possible that Captain Fulcher had 'borrowed' what he needed from one of Mr Partington's hoards? And what if the old man should discover that he had?

She dared not suggest to him now that the Captain, too, might know his secret. He had taken the news that she and the twins had learnt it badly enough. To find that a man like Jack Fulcher had some idea of the existence of all that gold might be the death of him indeed.

'Well, sir,' she said, wondering how long she had stood in front of him lost in these thoughts. 'Well, sir, I have told you what I have learnt, as I thought my duty. May I add just this? That I trust you will see to it that the money there, such as it is, is removed to another place which neither myself nor Maria nor Louisa know of, and that I shall do my best to forget that I ever saw what I did.'

This last, however, was a promise she knew she could hardly keep. The sight of those piles and piles of sovereigns glinting in the flickering light from the girls' stub of candle was not something she could easily banish from her mind.

But she would try to act as if she had. That at least she could do.

The old man made no reply.

She turned to go.

Her hand was on the wooden knob of the door when from behind her she heard a croak of sound, hardly a spoken word. She looked back.

'Miss.'

That was what the old miser had forced from between those loose and yellowy teeth.

'Yes, sir?'

'There is something I – Something I wish to say.'

The words were whispered, hoarsely whispered and hardly audible. Little though she liked doing it, Miss Unwin took a chair and placed it up close to Mr Partington's desk. She sat and leant forward till she was in

46

a position to hear clearly what it was the old miser might have to say – and to receive in its full unpleasantness the whiff of his breath from those dark blue gums.

She listened intently.

'How did it come about? How? How did it happen?'

With a lurch of dismay she realised that, far from herself coming to the miser with a confession for which he would dart his fiercest anger at her, she was on the point of hearing a confession from him.

It could be nothing else. The words whispered in foul breath across the scuffed leather of the desk were searching, self-searching.

Every question that she had asked herself about the old man must be echoing now in his own head. How had he brought himself to deprive his own son of even a shilling to pay a governess's cab fare? How could he keep his grandchildren in such unnecessary penury that they had never in the nine years of their existence so much as entered a sweetshop? How could he half-starve himself and his dependants in the way that he did?

Would she hear the answers to those questions now?

Chapter Five

Miss Unwin made herself sit as still as she might wish of any of her pupils on their best behaviour and waited to hear what the old miser would have to say. She feared she was going to have to listen to an account she would rather not have to hear. During every meeting with her employer in the days to come she would have the knowledge of his utmost weakness in her mind. And he would have the knowledge that she knew in his.

But there was no escaping. The old man had embarked on his confession and all she could do was to hear him out as self-effacingly as possible.

'How did it happen? How did I come to this? I was a happy man once. Yes, I see you shake your head in disbelief.'

Miss Unwin had not moved so much as a muscle.

'I see you shake your head in disbelief, but once, years ago, many years ago, I was as happy a man as you could find in all London, a carefree happy fellow. And in the full first flush of delightful married life.'

The old man fell silent.

Miss Unwin sat on, unmoving as a painted picture. She had learnt in bitterness in her earliest workhouse days the value of sitting so still that watchful eyes passed on over her, and she had lost nothing of the trick.

But she thought. She realised that never once in the weeks she had spent as governess of Richard Partington's children had she asked herself what Richard's own mother had been like. Old Mr Partington, that grotesque figure with the short, wasted body and the huge looming head, had seemed to her somehow a creature who had always existed in the form that she daily saw him. Despite the evidence of his son, hale and hearty, she had not once wondered how Richard had come into the world.

And now, with absolute unexpectedness, she was being given an account of the long ago marriage that had produced, not another monster, but a son of charm and modesty.

'She died,' the old miser suddenly resumed, in his dreadful breathy whisper. 'She had carried to full time our first-born, the babe I knew would be my son. And within a day of his birth she lay dead. Dead. Dead. Dead.'

Abruptly under the mask of her stillness Miss Unwin felt her heart bound in sympathy. In sympathy for the impossibly mean man who had systematically made her life a shiveringly cold and hungry torment ever since she had entered his house. In sympathy for the man who had not only made her life so chill and drab but had made the lives of her two young charges, those creatures endowed with hope and liveliness, equally chill, equally drab. But the thought that not only had his loved wife died in giving birth to his only son but that that son's wife had in turn died in giving birth to the twins struck at her now till she felt the tears ready to gush.

Yet she held them back. She knew she must. Soon the old man who was recalling his early misery to her would regret with redoubled sharpness that he had ever spoken. Now all she could do to make him doubt at any future time just how much he had bared his soul was to sit and will herself into immobility, into nothingness.

'Yes,' the old miser went on. 'Yes, the wife of my delight died. And, if you will believe me, until that day I had not thought of a future at all. Young, foolish as I was I had lived as if nothing would ever change. As if happiness was a thing that lasted. As if it was not such as to be blasted to mere shards in a moment.'

Miss Unwin sat and listened and willed herself yet more into immobility.

'But I came away from that death bed with my lesson learnt,' the old man continued. 'That much I will say for myself. I did not take long to learn that hard, hard lesson. And I resolved at that hour, at that very minute, that what I could do to protect myself from such another blow I would do. Yes, illness could strike at me. The cholera. The influenza. But from all which prudence could save me I would be saved. And you know, do you not, what is the one thing that can protect? The one thing?'

Till then he had been communing not with any person in that cramped room but with a ghostly confessor, perhaps in his mind. But at this question he turned to Miss Unwin, statue-still on the chair beside his desk, and put the words to her with entire directness.

She knew then that she had to answer. She had to acknowledge that she herself was indeed present. Was present to be remembered ever afterwards.

'Yes, sir,' she said. 'I suppose I do know what it is that you will believe will protect you from such troubles as we can be protected from. It is gold, is it not? The gold you have stored away?'

The old man looked at her, his eyes once again taking on their look of malevolent cunning.

'You know where it is,' he said softly. 'You know.'

Miss Unwin felt herself in danger then. In danger as surely as if at the Zoological Gardens she had stepped somehow into a cage of snakes.

'Sir,' she said, 'it is true that I did by a fearful mischance come upon some of the gold you feel to be so necessary to you. But I have asked you to move that wealth to some other place of concealment, and I know that you will do so and that I shall no longer have the least inkling of your secret.'

She expected some sharp denial of the possibility of any

51

such deliberating. And indeed she recognised that she was once again promising something hardly in human nature to perform. But the response she got was very different.

'I must have it,' the old man said. 'I must have safety. You would not deny me that? Add to add, add to add, it is the only way. Add to add and add to add, and it adds to safety at the last.'

Miss Unwin thought at one time that this pronouncing of his creed was to be the last words the old miser ever spoke. Because, no sooner had he uttered them, leaning yet more forward towards her, than he gave a single high-pitched scream of pain, wrapped both arms round his stomach in an uncontrollable gesture and fell forward on the desk in front of her, unconscious.

Miss Unwin, after a moment of shocked inability to move, rose from her chair, felt at the old man's forehead, gathered from the damp heat there that he was not dead, for all that the extreme agony of this bout might have meant it had been fatal, and hurried at once to summon assistance.

The clerk, whom she had spoken to at the top of the stairs, proved to be a person not easily flustered. He summoned two hulking fellows from the machines below and between them they carried the old man across to the house and laid him on his bed.

Little of those minutes remained clear in Miss Unwin's head afterwards. But she recalled with a sort of pity seeing how bare and chill the old man's bedroom was, no more comfortable than her own small chamber on the floor above. And, later still, she realised that the bed on to which the two operatives had lowered that little body was plainly still the marriage bed where, some thirty years before, a young wife had died after childbirth and that old man had, looking down at her lifeless corpse, resolved on his course of ever-gathering penny-pinching.

But even while she was wondering, as the two burly operatives dipping and ducking left the room, whether

52

she should send for medical assistance and indeed whom she should send for the old man's eyelids fluttered open.

Miss Unwin approached more closely to the bed.

'Sir,' she said, 'you are gravely ill. You collapsed while we were talking at the works and have been carried back here. Please tell me who is your physician. I am certain he ought to be summoned.'

'Oh, yes,' came the feeble croaking reply. 'Summoned to hold out his hand for his seven shillings and sixpence. No, I want no doctor.'

'But, sir –'

'No, I tell you. No. Leave me to rest and in an hour I shall be as right as ever I was.'

'Very well, sir, I will send for no one,' Miss Unwin answered, wary of provoking perhaps yet another attack. 'But let me at least stay with you until your son returns.'

She received no answer to that, and took it for agreement.

So for an hour more she sat in the old miser's bare room and watched over him as he lay, eyes closed, occasionally giving a quiet groan but otherwise silent. At the end of the hour Richard Partington came in, having gone back to the pin works and heard what had happened. His open round face wore a look of sharp worry. Miss Unwin felt at once more sorry for him than she was for his father.

But she knew, too, that in telling him what had happened she must take the greatest care not to let slip the reason for this latest attack, to give no hint of what it was she herself had had to go to see the old man about.

Luckily Richard was so concerned that he failed to ask why she had been at the works when the attack had occurred.

'Your father is insistent that no doctor should be called,' she said in the quiet whisper of the sick room as they stood together at its door.

Richard frowned.

'He ought to have medical attention,' he said. 'I know

that he ought. These attacks are becoming increasingly frequent. But –'

He broke off. Yet Miss Unwin had no difficulty in completing his sentence in her head. *But he is as obstinate as the devil, and I do not dare cross him.*

Instead she asked an almost meaningless, soothing question. The answer she got was to give her, later, much food for thought. But at the time it did not at all occur to her that it was more than a reply equally soothing to both of them.

'How long is it that these attacks have been occurring?' she asked.

'Oh, not for very long,' Richard answered. 'He was as healthy as could be until a year or so ago. Otherwise I should never have left him to go and stay with Miss Fulcher down at Stavely.'

'No, I am sure that you would not,' Miss Unwin replied, thinking at that moment no more of it.

They stood for a while in silence. The heavy breathing of the sick man was all too easy to hear.

At last Richard spoke again.

'But what if he should die?' he asked. 'What if he should die and I have done nothing to bring him medical assistance?'

Miss Unwin hardly knew what response to make. Part of her wanted to say that old Mr Partington would not die, that Richard was right to heed his request not to have a doctor. But another part of her knew that the old man was terribly ill. He could die at any time, and if he did so without having had the benefit of medical advice the burden would lie heavy on his son.

She did not speak immediately in answer to his unspoken plea for comfort. And before she had found in her mind any reply to make he had voiced aloud another more urgent plea.

'Oh, Miss Unwin, you are the only person I feel I can trust in. Tell me what I should do.'

He reached forward then and grasped her hand.

Gently as she could she freed herself.

'Mr Partington, I cannot, whether I wish it or not, give you such advice. I am not the person you should ask.'

He made an effort to regain her hand, and this spurred her on to say what she had hesitated to add before.

'No, sir, if you must have advice, and I can see that you feel you must, there is someone – there is a lady who, surely, has the right to be asked for that assistance.'

'Miss Fulcher,' Richard answered dully. 'Cousin Cornelia. How can –'

'No, sir,' Miss Unwin broke in, answering more the dismissive tone of his voice than the words he had yet to utter. 'No, sir, I must not hear what you were about to say. I must not.'

Richard Partington fell silent then. They stood together in the gloom of the passageway outside the old man's bedroom.

At last Richard gave a long sigh.

'I suppose that once again I must go against my better judgment,' he said, 'and acquiesce in my father's decision. We will send for no medical assistance, and we will hope.'

Hope seemed answered in the days that followed. The old miser began gradually to recover from the attack, worse though it had been by far than any he had had before. When, at the end of a week in which he had kept his bed, once again Captain Fulcher and his sister were due to come to dine he announced that he would be present and would go back to the pin works next day.

'I dare say things will have got into a pretty state there,' Miss Unwin heard him say to his son as she made her way past his half-open door with her charges. 'You never had a head for business.'

'No, father, I suppose I have not. At least I have never disguised from you that it is an occupation I dislike.'

'But you are happy enough to live in idleness on what that business brings in, such as it is.'

55

'Come, father, I do not live in idleness.'

'I say you do, sir. Oh, I know that you sit at your desk during the hours of business. But you put no willingness into what you do. And you never have.'

'Well, father, I have not disguised from you either that I believe a manager could look after the works better than myself, and that they provide ample means to pay such a person and for both of us to live in comfort on the profits.'

'Comfort, comfort. You dare talk to me of comfort. I do not want comfort. And nor should you. There is something a deal more worth having than comfort.'

'And what is that, sir?'

Miss Unwin tried then to urge the twins onwards so that she might not hear the old miser's answer. Because she knew too well what it would be. But the girls had been fascinated by the dispute and were lingering unashamedly to hear more.

Miss Unwin gestured them onwards. But in vain. The word she had not wanted to hear was spoken.

'Safety,' came the old man's voice from behind the half-open door. 'Safety, you poor fool, that is what makes it all worth the doing. Safety. Safety. Safety.'

Miss Unwin put a hand to the small of Maria's back and another to Louisa and pushed.

Safety, safety, safety. The old miser's words rang in her ears as she urged the girls into their room. But she did not know then that they were to be all but the last she would hear him speak.

Chapter Six

Miss Unwin had not expected that she would see old Mr Partington downstairs early, though she had been ready to find him in the dining room with the Fulchers when she came down with the twins for dinner. But he was absent. Richard, too, was not in the room. Presumably he was still assisting his father to dress.

So Miss Unwin had the task of making polite conversation to the Fulchers, especially since she thought it important to avoid the twins attacking the Captain once more. It was, after all, possible that he had not yet listened acutely enough to their teasing prattle to have discovered from it Mr Partington's secret. If that were so, whatever she could do to keep that state of affairs she must.

'I am afraid, Miss Fulcher, you will find Mr Partington very much less well than at the time of your last visit,' she said.

Miss Fulcher's thin, raw-red nose lifted disparagingly.

'The air of London. Little wonder that Mr Partington does not keep good health.'

'I am afraid that it is worse than that,' Miss Unwin allowed herself to answer with some sharpness. 'Mr Partington suffered a grave seizure a week ago. He became unconscious. We had to carry him from the works to his bed, and he is leaving that only now.'

'All work and no play,' Captain Fulcher boomed in. 'Always said toiling away at a damned desk did a fellow no good.'

'It was not his toil that brought on the attack,' Miss Unwin answered, yet more sharply.

At once she regretted the remark.

'Not his toil?' Cousin Cornelia said. 'Then, pray, Miss, what was the cause of the onset?'

'It was – It was –'

Miss Unwin sought inspiration. And found it in the nick of time.

'It appears to have been something he had eaten,' she said.

'Eaten, eh?' Captain Fulcher brayed. 'Shouldn't have thought the fellow ever ate enough to do anybody any harm. Or drank enough.'

He turned abruptly away and began to open the two bottles of sherry which in his customary way he had brought with him.

'And where is my dear Cousin Richard?' Miss Fulcher asked with a fearful simper.

Miss Unwin thought of the sharply certain way in which only a week before, when they had been so concerned about old Mr Partington's refusal of a doctor, Richard had rejected the idea of Cousin Cornelia being the person from whom he ought above all to ask advice.

'I expect he is assisting his father,' she answered. 'I am afraid that Mr Partington –'

She broke off.

On the stairs outside there had come the sound of urgent pounding steps. A moment later the door was flung open and Richard stood there, white faced.

'Father, father,' he said. 'I – I think that – that he may be dead.'

Cousin Cornelia took a step backwards away from him. From her brother there came a snorted 'Well, really.'

Miss Unwin decided at once that she must see for herself what the old man's state really was. Richard had said only that he might be dead.

She brushed past him as he stood, still holding the knob of the door he had thrust open, visibly trembling with shock. She took the stairs at an unladylike run and without ceremony went straight into the old man's room.

She found him lying on the floor, and for an instant she thought that a last attack had indeed laid him low. But before she had time even to kneel and examine the little, half-dressed body a faint groan came.

Carefully as she could she rolled the old miser over. The sight of his face made her think that, if he was living still, he could not be far from the end. Even the projecting ears on either side of the enormous white skull were now devoid of colour while the rest of his countenance was an appalling grey.

She began to chafe his hands, not knowing what else there was that could be done.

After a little she became aware that Richard had broken free of the trance that seemed to have struck him after he had made his announcement in the dining room. He was standing looking down at her.

'What happened?' she asked, continuing to rub and rub at the old man's icy hands.

'I feared he was not well,' Richard answered. 'He seemed so lethargic when he tried to dress. But he was adamant that he would come down to dine. He said –'

Richard checked as if some thick scarf had been wrapped suddenly across his mouth.

'He said,' he went on at last in a curiously hollow voice, 'that if I was too weak to win Cousin Cornelia for myself he would see to the business for me.'

Miss Unwin was aware that Richard had said what he ought never to have allowed himself to say. But before she could in her turn say a word to indicate that she had not heard him, or had not fully understood, she felt in the hand she held between her mechanically rubbing fingers a faint twitch.

'I believe he is recovering,' she said. 'Perhaps this may not be what we had feared.'

Certainly the old miser began to show further signs of life. His eyelids fluttered. A faint pinkness began to creep back into his lips. He stirred.

'Where – Where –'

'Hush,' Miss Unwin said. 'You had another attack, sir. You fell to the floor. But we can get you to bed again in a moment. You will be better there.'

The old man did not answer, and Miss Unwin resumed the vigorous chafing that had seemed to restore him.

After a little two more words came from his still almost bloodless lips.

'No – doctor.'

Miss Unwin turned from her task and looked up at Richard.

She saw a spasm of determination come over his face, transforming momentarily its pleasant roundness into something more active.

'No,' he said quietly to her, with the evident intention of not letting his father hear. 'No, this time I will do what I know I ought. I will go round myself at once to Doctor Sumsion.'

'Yes,' Miss Unwin answered. 'You are right. I am certain of it.'

She looked down at the old man. But his eyes were closed and it seemed he had not heard the words that might have sent him into a paroxysm of rage, perhaps fatally.

From behind her as she knelt she heard Richard's voice, with a note of plaintiveness in it.

'There is one thing . . .'

'Yes?'

'Miss Unwin, Harriet, you must know, you must have seen or guessed by now: my father never lets me have money. Not so much as a single penny. I – I can't pay the doctor his fee.'

Miss Unwin looked up at him over her shoulder. His face was simply woebegone.

'I am sure the doctor will not ask for money before he has examined your father,' she said.

'Oh, he may, he may. A year ago when the children had the measles my father refused him half of his seven shillings and sixpence, and he declared then that he would not attend anyone in this house unless he were paid beforehand.'

'Oh, very well,' Miss Unwin said, unable to keep a trace of impatience out of her voice. 'I have some small savings. I will produce what is necessary.'

'Oh, thank you, thank you. You have no idea –'

'You had better go at once,' Miss Unwin broke in. 'The least delay may mean you are too late.'

'Yes, Yes, you are right.'

Richard turned and she heard him running along the passage and tumbling almost down the stairs.

He proved not to be too late in fetching the doctor, and nor were his fears about the man's possible intransigence over his fee justified. Doctor Sumsion, for all his considerable age and rotundity of figure, did not hesitate for a moment when he saw old Mr Partington still lying on the floor where Miss Unwin had found him.

'Good gracious me,' he said. 'The poor fellow is *in extremis*. No doubt about that. No doubt at all.'

He took his stethoscope from out of the tall silk hat he held, knelt with a little grunt beside Miss Unwin and began his examination.

'Can we lift him on to his bed now, Doctor?' Miss Unwin asked when he had eventually finished.

'No. No, I think not.'

The doctor got laboriously to his feet and turned to address Richard.

'Mr Partington,' he said, 'unless I am very much mistaken your father will not rest on that bed again. I have to tell you that he has only minutes to live.'

'My gold.'

From the floor behind them the two words issued from

61

the lips of the dying miser. In a few moments they were repeated. 'My gold.'

Miss Unwin could not help feeling that they were words spoken from beyond the grave.

And they were the very last that the old man uttered. As the three of them stood helplessly looking down at him he gave one final short groan. The doctor dropped to his knees again beside him and applied his stethoscope.

'Yes,' he said. 'Yes. He has gone. Poor fellow, may the Lord have mercy upon his soul.'

Richard stepped forward to help him to his feet.

He stood for a long moment looking Richard full in the face.

Miss Unwin thought that he must simply be recovering his breath after the exertion and perhaps the inevitable shock, even for a medical man, of witnessing the moment of death. But she was soon disillusioned. The doctor had been in deep and perplexed thought. And at last he spoke.

'Mr Partington,' he said, 'I have to tell you that I am by no means happy over your father's demise. I have seen many men and women go to the great Beyond, and I know the symptoms of most illnesses as well as any man, though I say it.'

He fell silent, still looking Richard straight in the eye.

'Yes, sir,' he continued, 'I know what death from disease should look like. And those signs were not there with your father. But other signs there were. Unmistakable signs. Mr Partington, I believe your father died by poison. I cannot sign a death certificate. There will have to be a post-mortem examination.'

Chapter Seven

No sooner had puffing old Doctor Sumsion spoken the word 'poison' than into Miss Unwin's mind there came, vivid as a painting, a picture of the scene during the first parsimonious meal she had eaten in this chill house. She saw again the seven of them at the dining table, old Mr Partington at its head, Cousin Cornelia, honoured guest and though she herself had not known it at the time destined bride for Richard Partington, her brother Jack on old Mr Partington's other side, lounging in his chair and looking decidedly ill-tempered at the shortage of wine, the twins sitting opposite each other, shabby and subdued in their ill-washed frocks. Then herself, a wary and perplexed newcomer, and Richard Partington at the far end from his father, giving her from time to time rueful, awkward smiles, very conscious of the deficiencies of the household. And, just as they had finished eating the small helpings of meat and the wretched boiled potatoes that had accompanied them, old Mr Partington had had his second attack of griping internal pain that evening and in refusing medical attention had blurted out his accusation of poisoning.

Not once in the weeks she had been in the neglected, shabby house, as the weather had gradually warmed into spring and as old Mr Partington's attacks had continued at intervals, had she heard him make the accusation again. If she ever thought of it in those cold, cramped days, it had been to dismiss the words as the expression of a momentary malignant fury.

But now, with Doctor Sumsion's considered judgment

still ringing in her ears, she realised that, far from being some exasperated exaggeration, the accusation must have been true.

Mr Partington's attacks of violent pain had not been the symptoms of an illness he was suffering from. They had been signs that someone had been slowly and with evil intent trying to end his life.

Yet Miss Unwin could hardly credit it.

Why should anyone behave in a manner so fiendishly cruel? And, worse, could that person be, as would seem most likely, someone inside the house or a frequent visitor to it?

She decided there and then that she would pursue such thoughts no further. If Doctor Sumsion was correct in his diagnosis and this terrible thing had indeed taken place, it was at least no immediate concern of hers. She herself had been an ignorant witness of events in the house. None of them had meant anything to her. If the doctor's accusation, for that undoubtedly was what it was, was to be pursued it was a task for the proper authorities. No doubt Richard Partington would call them in, or the doctor would do so himself.

No doubt, too, in the coming days there would be a great deal of unpleasantness while the investigations were carried out, and she herself would come in for some share of it. But the investigations and anything they might bring to light were truly no real concern of hers.

What was her concern was the two children who had at this moment been deprived of their grandfather. There was no use in pretending that they had loved the old man. He was not lovable. But he was part of their lives and the suddenness of his death would come as a shock. For that she must prepare them, and in the coming weeks she must do all she could to help them over its effects and to protect them from those inquiries that were bound to be made.

That and no more.

But Miss Unwin was to find almost at once that her role

64

in the house could not be confined simply to looking after the two little girls who were her responsibility.

As she left the room where old Mr Partington lay dead and went to find Louisa and Maria to break the sad news to them, both Richard Partington and Doctor Sumsion came downstairs. So she was in the bare hall when the doctor, with a little 'Hem' of embarrassment, put a request to the new master of the establishment.

'There is one small matter, my dear sir. I hesitate to mention it at such a time, but the affairs of this world must proceed.'

Richard blinked at him, absolutely without understanding.

But Miss Unwin had grasped the meaning of the doctor's roundabout words at once. He wanted to make sure of his fee.

First she remembered her hasty promise that from her small savings she would find, if necessary, the seven shillings and sixpence which a doctor would require sooner or later as the case might be. She could run up to her room at this moment, take the coins from the box in which she kept her savings and – And then what? It would greatly embarrass Richard if she were to give him the sum in front of the doctor, thus betraying the fact that his father had kept him deprived of even the smallest coin.

But with that reflection came, pouring in, another. Richard's father was no longer holding the purse strings. Richard himself was now the heir to all the old man's wealth.

Then yet another thought crowded in. All the old miser's wealth was in the form of gold, of gold concealed here and there in this very house. And of that Richard, she was almost certain, knew nothing.

But this was no moment to ponder the implications of all the secret knowledge she herself had. There was an immediate dilemma facing the new master of the house.

And she saw at once how she could help him.

'I think, sir,' she said, going over to him, 'that Doctor Sumsion would like to receive his fee. May I go and fetch the necessary sum for you? I know where you keep money for immediate use.'

It took Richard, visibly, some moments to understand what she had said. But at last he answered.

'Why, yes. Yes. Yes, Miss Unwin, that would be very kind. I – I am afraid I am somewhat discomposed. Thank you. Thank you.'

It was a look of real gratitude that he gave her as she turned to go.

Yet it was as nothing compared to the flood of realisation which spread over his open round face some half an hour later when, with the difficult business of telling Louisa and Maria of their loss and indeed making them appreciate that it was a loss completed, she informed him of the great wealth that lay literally under his feet.

'Miss Unwin, Harriet, how – how can I thank you? To know so much, to have found it out. To have kept the secret, to tell it to me now, now that it can mean so much to me. I do not know how to thank you enough. Yes. Yes, by Jove, I do. Ask me for something, Miss Unwin, Harriet. Ask. Please ask. Ask for anything. Help me to show how grateful I am, shall always be. Yes, ask. Ask. Please ask.'

The wild tumbling of words might have made Miss Unwin laugh aloud had the circumstances been otherwise. But she thought of the old man lying dead in the room above them. She thought how only an hour or so before he had been alive, though ill indeed. And she thought, too, that Richard Partington had been calling her Harriet. This was something he ought not to have done. She must be, she could never be otherwise to him than, plain Miss Unwin, governess.

Whatever, in the clash of wild emotions that were meeting in him at this moment, he might imagine.

'Mr Partington,' she said with haste, 'I do not ask you to believe me about what I have told you. It is in truth almost unbelievable. But come with me now and I will show you where I saw that hidden store of gold, where Louisa and Maria led me to it. Your father has been in no condition to remove it since the time he learnt from me that his secret was known.'

'Yes. Yes. Show me. Please. But – but of course I believe you. You are a person I should never disbelieve.'

'Come with me, Mr Partington,' Miss Unwin replied, forcing herself to be stern almost as a gaoler.

She led Richard Partington at once and hastily down to the basement and, recognising instantly the thin flagstone which she had watched her two charges replace in the late hours of the night only a week earlier, she knelt to raise it up.

But hardly had she done so when a voice came harshly cackling out from behind her.

'Thief. Thief. Stop that. Stop. Taking a sick man's gold. Stop it, you thieves.'

It was Mrs Meggs.

She stood there in the doorway from the kitchen a more than ever malevolent figure, the eyes in her dark brown face glittering with fury, the sole bristly white hair jutting from her chin seemingly more prominent than ever.

Miss Unwin realised then that in all the turmoil of old Mr Partington's death, in her trouble over telling the two girls, in the complications of explaining what had happened to Captain Fulcher and his sister, in seeing them leave, dinnerless, neither she nor Richard had thought to tell Mrs Meggs in the kitchen, busy over the last preparations for their scanty meal, what had happened.

'Mrs Meggs,' Richard said now, 'I must tell you that your Master is no longer alive. He died, quite suddenly, an hour since.'

'You lie, you lie!' the old woman screamed out. 'You

67

think you can rob him and pretend to me he is no more.'

'Mrs Meggs,' Richard said, 'I assure you I am speaking the simple truth. My father is dead. Doctor Sumsion was here and witnessed his end.'

'Yet you come to rob him before his breath is cool,' the old woman shouted back. 'I called you thief, and thief you are. You and that precious hussy of yours.'

Miss Unwin had not realised until this moment that the bad-tempered and mean-minded old housekeeper was quite as devoted to her employer, despite the way she had made sure he ate meat when all the rest of the household had vegetables only, despite the extra large cup she always gave him when it was time for tea. But now she saw the full extent of the link between the two aged and miserly people. And she saw something else, too. Mrs Meggs had got it into her head that Richard Partington took a special interest in herself.

Perhaps, she thought, it is true. He does in moments of stress call me Harriet. He did once at a hard time for himself ask me for advice about calling a doctor against his father's wishes. Yet . . . Yet surely he cannot truly feel for me anything that could cause a bad-tempered old crone like Mrs Meggs to think of me as his 'hussy'.

But Richard Partington evidently felt the jibe as going too near home.

'Mrs Meggs,' he said, 'you will apologise instantly to this lady. I know that the news you have just heard must have distressed you. I know that you have served my father for many, many years. But what you have said is unforgiveable. Apologise for it this instant.'

'Thief I have called you, and thief I have called her,' the old woman answered. 'And thieves you are, the pair of you. Stealing what the Master saved and scrimped for over the years, stealing it within an hour of his dying. You, Miss, are a thief, a thief and this man's whore.'

Richard Partington's simple round face went turkey-cock red.

'Go!' he thundered. 'Go. Leave this house, leave at once. I – I will give you what wages you are owed. But leave my house now you shall.'

'Wages!' the old woman screamed back at him. 'I am owed more than wages. I am owed under the Will. Dare you say different?'

'Very well then. I will pay you from this gold a sum that should satisfy you. But I will not tolerate your presence here one moment longer. Get out. Get out. Send for your possessions when you will, but be out of this house tonight.'

Miss Unwin, standing there confused and hurt by the violence of this sudden scene, wondered whether the vicious yet deprived old woman would obey. Would her hatred, her loss, be too strong?

But, somewhat to her surprise, the unexpected anger Richard Partington had shown had its effect. Mrs Meggs stepped back towards the kitchen.

'Yes, I'll go,' she said in an evil mutter. 'I'll shake the dust of this accursed house from me. But you will suffer, killer of your own father. You will suffer, don't fear for that.'

She turned then and scuttled away.

And barely half an hour later Miss Unwin saw her by the light of the nearest street lamp go stumping out of the house, a wicker basket seemingly all she cared to take with her.

But during the time between the ancient housekeeper uttering that final malediction and her departure Miss Unwin had had much to think about. The words the old woman had uttered had sent a dart of fear into her. *Killer of your own father*. And that very evening Doctor Sumsion had solemnly declared that in his considered opinion old Mr Partington had been killed, had been poisoned.

Could Mrs Meggs have suspected something of this? Certainly she had been present serving the meal on that first night she herself had spent in the house when Mr Partington had uttered his claim that he was being poisoned. And who was it that Mrs Meggs had accused? None other than the one person who had befriended her here, apart from her two charges. She had accused Richard Partington of killing his own father, and it was just possibly true that he had reason to kill a father who had treated him worse than the lowest servant. If ever there was reason for a son to murder a father, then perhaps Richard Partington did have such a reason.

She felt a chill of premonition rise up in her.

But it was dispelled at that instant. Richard, too, had been watching his father's old housekeeper and single servant stump away into the darkness.

'Well,' he said, coming up to stand at the uncurtained window beside Miss Unwin, 'to tell the truth I had long wished to see her go, though knowing how she cared for my father I would not have had her leave in this way and on this day.'

'No,' Miss Unwin answered. 'I, too, feel sorry for her, though she did nothing to make my life easy here.'

Richard gave a little laugh.

'At least,' he said, 'we shall no longer have to endure those fearful meals, though what we shall eat tonight I cannot imagine. And the girls certainly ought to have something.'

'As for tonight,' Miss Unwin replied, 'no doubt Mrs Meggs has left in the oven what we were intended to have for dinner, and, since it was meant for three more than will eat it, there will perhaps be enough. I can easily bring it to the table myself.'

'You are very good,' Richard answered. 'Indeed, so good that I –'

Miss Unwin thought it was time to interrupt. And an idea had occurred to her opportunely to put forward.

'Mr Partington,' she broke in, 'Mr Partington, since we

shall be without any servant now, may I make a suggestion?'

'Of course. I am sure any suggestion you may have will be more than sensible.'

'It is simply this then,' Miss Unwin hurried on. 'At my last place of employment there was a housemaid whose work was particularly good. I know she no longer wants to stay on in her present situation, so may I ask her if she would care to come here? Her name is Vilkins, Mary Vilkins. I have known her a long time.'

Indeed, she thought privately, I have known poor Vilkins as long as it is possible for any two people to have known each other. Were we not brought to the parish workhouse one after the other as foundlings, I to be named Unwin and she following me to receive the name which that ignorant beadle believed was spelt with the next letter in the alphabet?

She thought then how in the new awkward circumstances that she foresaw facing her it would be a comfort to have dear Vilkins with her. To have well-meaning, clumsy Vilkins, her broad face with its ever-red dab of a nose well to the fore, beside her.

'Why, of course,' said Richard Partington. 'Perhaps tomorrow as early as may be you could go back to Bayswater and ask her if she is willing to take a post with us. And – And tell her the wages she will receive will be handsome, more than handsome. I have the means now, and I will use them to the full.'

Chapter Eight

Miss Unwin hardly took in Richard Partington's words as he told her that she could bring to the house Vilkins, her old friend if social inferior now. Mostly she was simply pleased at the prospect. She greatly feared difficult times lay ahead. There was to be the post-mortem examination of old Mr Partington's body, and if that revealed, as Doctor Sumsion had seemed sure that it would, that the old miser had indeed died by poison then there would be a police inquiry.

It would be an inquiry that would, at the very best, be acutely distressing. But, if those wild words which Mrs Meggs had uttered before she left the house had meant anything, an investigation could be far worse than distressing. It would mean that Richard Partington would fall under suspicion, and in the weeks in which she had been governess to his children Miss Unwin had conceived a very great liking for Richard. He had borne up well, she believed, under appalling circumstances. Persecuted by his excessively mean father, he had smiled and not lost his temper and had tried and tried to make the best of things.

What other man, she had asked herself often, would endure those empty pockets? And this was the person who might well be accused by wagging tongues, if by no others, of the terrible crime of patricide.

So Richard Partington's offer of more than handsome wages for Vilkins, contrasting sharply as it did with his father's insistence not so many weeks before that she herself should accept a salary which many a servant would have refused with disdain, passed by her entirely.

Even the realisation of just how wealthy her employer now was had scarcely impinged on her. During the evening they had together searched the old dingy house for Mr Partington's other hiding-places. There had been no fewer than five of them. Two more under flagstones in the basement – Miss Unwin by carefully pacing to and fro had been able to detect where a stone slightly wobbled – two behind loose pieces of wainscot in the dining room and in the little parlour, and a last one, the only one not full-packed with softly gleaming sovereigns, in the old man's bedroom under a floorboard on which the greasy marks of his scrabbling fingers could still be made out.

There had not been enough time even to count every coin that night. But between them they had roughly calculated that Richard Partington was now possessed of a fortune more than double that which his rich Cousin Cornelia had inherited. He was, indeed, suddenly a man of gold, little though she properly had taken it in.

So when Miss Unwin went early next day as Richard had suggested and put his offer of employment to Vilkins she did vaguely recall that something had been mentioned about wages and thought herself empowered to say to Vilkins that she would be paid not less than she was receiving in Bayswater. But in any case Vilkins had been so joyful at the prospect of the two of them being under the same roof again that she had brushed aside all question of money.

'Oh, Unwin, we'll have such larks. Such larks we'll have when their backs is turned an' we can remember what we was in the old days.'

'The bad old days, Vilkins, my dear. Remember that.'

'Oh, lawks, yes, bad they was. Hungry we was and cold like what we never ain't been since.'

'As to that, I'm not so sure,' Miss Unwin replied with a smile. 'I tell you I have been cold enough since I left here, and hungry too.'

'What, ain't I a-going to get me dinners in the place where you are?'

Miss Unwin smiled again.

'I think I can promise you you'll get as good a dinner now as in any servants' hall anywhere,' she said. 'But while the old gentleman who was head of the house was alive we had short commons enough, all of us, in the dining room as well as in the kitchen.'

But the dinners Vilkins got proved, in fact, to be a good deal better than in most servants' halls. And the meals, prepared by a new cook, that she brought up to the dining room were nothing other than luxurious. Richard Partington was spending the gold he had taken from its hiding-place by the basement door and in the other places in the house as if each sovereign were no more than a penny.

He bought himself new clothes. Miss Unwin was quite ready to acknowledge that the old blue coat and the old green trousers in which she had first seen him, and in which she had seen him every day that she had been in the house, deserved to be discarded. They had been turned by a tailor long ago, she had soon spotted, and their former insides had become as lacking in nap as, no doubt, their old outsides had once been. But the number of new coats and the pairs and pairs of trousers that he had made for himself astonished her.

Yet he did not buy for himself only. Maria and Louisa, for so long dressed in the cheapest of calico frocks, were given new ones by the dozen, and in silk. Nor were clothes all that was lavished on them. The painters were ordered in to make their joint bedroom, once drab almost as a prison cell, into as pretty a chamber as could be imagined. Two little white beds were bought from the upholsterer's, their white curtains looped back with knots of pink ribbon. Two pretty white toilet tables were installed, each with its cargo of trinkets, little mother-of-pearl-backed looking-glasses, vases for flowers, and a tiny bell of silver each with which to summon poor Vilkins who, to tell true, made clumsy work of acting the ladies' maid.

But that service, in any case, was something which Miss Unwin discouraged. The girls had made their own toilets until this time, and there was no reason, she felt, why they should not go on doing so for the most part, even though the clothes they had were finer and the brushes with which they brushed their hair had silver backs in place of the single wooden-backed one they had had to share in the days when they had lived, unjustly, like paupers.

Nor was Miss Unwin herself forgotten in the golden shower. Indeed, before long she felt bound to protest in strong terms as with each succeeding evening Richard Partington came back with some new gift, a bracelet in coral, a silver-gilt pencil-case, or simply a cake from the pastrycook's whirled round with pink cream.

'No, sir,' she said, when Richard attempted to fasten the little pencil-case by its chain round her wrist. 'No employer should give anyone in his employ such things as this.'

'But it gives me pleasure to do so.'

'Yes, sir, I can see that it does that, and I can understand it. After so many years of deprivation it is little wonder that you should enjoy the fruits of wealth and enjoy bestowing them on others.'

'Then let me bestow this pencil-case – it is but a trifle – on you, Harriet.'

'No, sir. Well, if you must I will accept it as a last gift. But on one condition.'

'And what is that, you iron maiden?'

'Sir, I do not wish to have to say this. But I must. You force me to. Sir, it is not proper that you should call me other than Miss Unwin, and I beg you not to do otherwise in the future.'

'But – But –'

The expression of perplexity on his cheerful, snub-nosed face was comical to see. Miss Unwin well knew from it what was passing through his mind. One half of him, she did not doubt, was wanting to insist on calling her by the forbidden forename. The other half was willing to please her by doing as she had asked. And she thought, that second half knew, too, that what she had said was right. He ought not to be taking such a liberty with her. Not unless he meant more by it than in his position he should.

'Come, Mr Partington,' she said. 'Please me in this, as much as you pleased me by your gift. Promise me that for the whole time I am in this house, however long or short it may be, you will address me as you ought to address your children's governess.'

Richard hesitated.

He looked down at the carpet at his feet. It was new, had been installed only two days before, a luxurious Turkey with a pattern of roses. Miss Unwin was aware suddenly of the particular smell of a new carpet in her nostrils, like fresh straw.

'Oh, very well, if you really do insist,' Richard said at last. 'But, all the same, tell me, please, why you speak of your stay here as being possibly short. You do not mean to leave me? To leave us, I should say.'

'No, sir, I have no intention of leaving while I can help Maria and Louisa in any way.'

'Then why this talk of a short stay? I mean, you – Well, never mind what I mean for the present. Why a short stay, Miss Unwin?'

Now it was Miss Unwin's turn to hesitate in answering. But it was not her nature to fudge an issue.

'Sir, it is because you yourself may not stay in this house for very long.'

'You think I may buy something else? I have thought of it, but I am not sure, now that I come to it, that I want to live anywhere other than in the house where I was born.'

'I am glad to hear that, sir.'

Miss Unwin rejected an easy way out, and gathered her courage again.

'But that is not what I meant.'

'Then what did you mean? I'm blessed if I know.'

'Well, sir, is it not possible that you will, before many months have passed, be residing at Stavely?'

It was said. Miss Unwin felt a burden lifted.

'At Stavely? With Cousin Cornelia? As Cousin Cornelia's husband? Oh, Harr– Oh, Miss Unwin, the idea is laughable.'

Miss Unwin found, to her enormous surprise, that Richard Partington's dismissal of the idea of marrying his cousin and going to live in the country sent a bound of emotion rising up in her. She was not at all sure what emotion it was. Joy? Relief? Mere wonder? But she knew she had felt it, and that she had been shaken by it.

'Then, sir,' she said, after what to her had seemed a long, long interval, 'I trust my stay in this house will not be short. I trust I shall find myself here perhaps until the girls' sixteenth birthday, unless –'

She checked herself at once. But the word had been spoken. The possibility that had come into her mind, perhaps because of the secret anxiety that had been satisfied only a moment before, had induced her to pronounce that one extra unnecessary word.

She hoped fervently that Richard Partington had not paid it any heed.

But he had.

'Unless? Unless what? It is my earnest hope that you will stay under my roof for . . . that you will certainly stay as the girls' governess as long as they need a governess.'

'Then we are in agreement at least over that,' Miss Unwin said.

And she turned to go.

'No, wait. Wait, Harr– Miss Unwin, one moment. You said that you hoped to stay here unless . . . There was an urgency in your tone. Unless what, Miss Unwin?'

For the second time in this brief interview Miss Unwin was at a loss how to reply. She had hesitated over telling Richard Partington that she believed he was to marry his cousin. Now she hesitated yet more about confessing to him the terrible thought that had risen unbidden to her mind when she had imagined her future in this house. The thought that she could not stay if its head was put on trial for murder and found guilty.

That was not a possibility that she believed in. Indeed, with all her will she wanted to thrust it away. But it had lain there waiting to leap out of ambush ever since Doctor Sumsion had given it as his opinion that old Mr Partington had been poisoned.

What was she going to say now in face of Richard Partington's insistence that she tell him what she had been going unwittingly to blurt out?

She was going to tell him the truth.

'Mr Partington, sir. Unless by some appalling chance it is thought –'

'It is thought what, Miss Unwin?'

On Richard Partington's face there was nothing but a guileless interest in what she was about to say. Not a trace of guilt trying to hide, not a trace even of guessing what it was that was in her mind. And yet . . . And yet it was all she could do to bring out the words she knew she must pronounce.

'Sir, unless by some chance too terrible to contemplate it is believed that you yourself are responsible for the death of your father.'

He stepped back a pace.

'But – But me. My father. What can you be saying?'

Innocence seemed written on every pore of his round open face. Miss Unwin could have sworn that the idea that he himself might be thought to be responsible for the poisoning of old Mr Partington had never once entered his head.

Yet even as she told herself this, the simple unswerving

sense of logic that had been implanted in her mind by one of her unknown parents made her realise that in trusting to what she had immediately felt about Richard she was trusting only in an impression. Logic said, inexorably, that if he had in fact poisoned his father he would have had to assume just such a look of scandalised innocence at the mention by anybody of the possibility.

However, she must seem to trust him. She owed him that. And she wanted passionately to be able to give him her trust without the reservation that her mind had forced her to make.

'Mr Partington,' she said in haste. 'Can it be that since Doctor Sumsion told you that he suspected your father had died by poison you have not considered how that poison can have been administered? Have you not thought how others might think it had been administered? Mr Partington, they will look to the one who most plainly benefits from your father's death. And – And –'

She faltered now for an instant. But she brought herself to resume.

'And, sir, since your father died you have been spending the money that he had saved over so many years as if – as if it was as freely come by as water from a well.'

'Yes. Yes, it is true. I have. But – But money is there to be spent, Miss Unwin. What else is it for? What good does it do if it is no more than pieces of gold, than pieces of some metal, hidden in the ground? Or in the vaults of a bank, which comes to much the same thing?'

'No, sir,' Miss Unwin answered steadily. 'I fear you should not think of it in that way. Yes, it is to be spent when it will buy what is necessary or even what is pleasant. But it is to be saved too, surely? Saved for worse times that may come.'

Richard smiled suddenly then, that old, disarming, wry smile which since the need for it had passed with his father's passing Miss Unwin had not seen.

'I suppose you are right,' he said. 'But, you know, I

80

have learnt to be prejudiced against the man who saves. Sadly I have learnt that.'

'Well, I can hardly blame you for that, sir,' Miss Unwin said.

And she meant those to be the words which would end this tempestuous conversation. Only at that moment the door of the drawing room, so newly furnished, was jerked open and Vilkins stood there.

'It's a caller,' she said.

Miss Unwin winced mentally. Her good friend certainly had little idea how a parlour-maid should behave. But then until now she had never aspired to any position in the long domestic hierarchy higher than that of a housemaid, a sweeper of carpets, layer of fires, duster of shelves, polisher of wood, maker of beds.

'A caller, Mary,' she said, for she had of course told nothing of the friendship between herself and Vilkins to Richard Partington and saw no need ever to do so. 'Is it a gentleman? Should you not have brought him in to wait in the hall?'

'Oh, it ain't no gentleman, Miss,' Vilkins replied cheerfully. 'He told me 'is name. It's the doctor. Doctor Somesing he said he was.'

'Doctor Sumsion?' said Richard Partington. 'What can he want?'

But Miss Unwin thought she knew. The post-mortem examination of old Mr Partington's body had already been delayed exceptionally long. It was more than likely that now the work had been done. Doctor Sumsion, whose patient in a sense old Mr Partington had been, was likely to have been present, and was likely now to be coming to inform Richard Partington of the findings.

'Mary, show the doctor up,' she said.

As soon as Vilkins had left, closing the door behind her with a hearty bang, Miss Unwin turned to Richard Partington.

'The examination of your father's body,' she said. 'I

imagine whatever tests were necessary have now been carried out.'

Again Richard, the innocent, looked surprised.

'Yes,' he said slowly. 'Yes, I suppose you are right. In which case we shall know all about it in just a few minutes.'

Abruptly his eyes glowed with sudden warmth.

'Miss Unwin,' he said, 'do not leave me. Stay here. I shall feel happier hearing whatever I will have to hear in your presence.'

'I am not sure –' she began.

But before she could express her doubts about the propriety of what he had asked the door was shoved open again and Vilkins put her head round it.

'It's the doctor,' she said. 'An' I forgot to say. There's another gentleman with 'im. Or not a gentleman rightly, either. He's the police.'

Chapter Nine

Miss Unwin hardly had eyes for Doctor Sumsion when he came into the room in the wake of Vilkins's extraordinary announcement. Even though she knew he was going to tell Richard Partington the result of the post-mortem examination, she had realised from the very fact that he was accompanied by a police officer that poison must have indeed been found in old Mr Partington's body. But what she feared more was that the police had already come to the conclusion that Richard must be responsible for its being there.

And this time he was not innocently unaware of what was happening. When she gave him a quick look she saw that his ordinarily cheerful red face had turned a lustreless grey.

The man who had entered half a pace behind the rotund physician spoke first.

'Your domestic has failed to name me,' he said. 'Inspector Redderman, Harrow Road Station.'

Miss Unwin looked at him.

He gave her at once the impression of being a man pared down to essentials. Later, thinking about him as she was to have cause enough to do, she was unable to account exactly for the vividness of her first strong feeling. It might have been, she thought, the clothes he wore, a suit of blue serge on which not a quarter-inch of material appeared to have been wasted. Or it might have been the set of his features where the flesh, again, seemed to have been distributed so as to serve its function of covering the bones beneath just to the necessary point and no more. Or it might have been the hair on his head which was trimmed back as far as it could be and still remain hair.

Yet none of these things had particularly struck her at first sight. However, the impression she had received was strong and it made her, though she could not in logic see why, somehow all the more apprehensive about the man.

It was characteristic of him, she later thought, that once he had told them who he was he added not a word more.

It was left to old Doctor Sumsion to reveal the purpose of their joint visit. And this, all too evidently, he was finding it hard to do.

He coughed once or twice. He darted a look at Miss Unwin which indicated both that he wished she was not in the room and that he was doubtful about just how he could rid himself of her presence.

Seeing his dilemma she felt bound to offer once again to go.

'Sir,' she said to Richard Partington, 'I believe Doctor Sumsion must have private business with you. I will take my leave.'

'No,' Richard Partington almost shouted. 'No, Miss Unwin, please, I particularly wish you to remain, whatever it may be that Doctor Sumsion and this gentleman have to say.'

He paused, then grabbed at a thought.

'Er – It is in the interest of my girls that you should be fully aware of the circumstances, of any circumstances, don't you see?'

'Very well, sir. If it is in the children's interest.'

Miss Unwin turned to the doctor and without actually saying anything made it clear that he had now to begin.

He coughed again.

'Very good, Mr Partington, if that is your wish,' he said. 'But I must warn you, however, that what I have to say is – is of the most intimate nature.'

But say it, for heaven's sake, Miss Unwin thought.

'No, no. Speak, speak,' Richard said.

84

'Very well. Then what I have to tell you is simply this: I have myself been conducting the post-morten examination on your father's body. Such work is something in which I have always taken the keenest interest. The examination is now completed. It was necessary to make certain tests on – organs removed. That is what has accounted for a certain delay.'

'But what has been found?' Richard barked out, impatience bringing the blood back to his ashen cheeks.

'Arsenic.'

It was the laconic Inspector Redderman who, at last, spoke the word.

'Arsenic?' Richard said. 'Poison? Then it is confirmed what you suspected, Doctor? My father was poisoned?'

'Yes,' the doctor answered with a tremendous expression of gravity. 'Yes, I regret to tell you that there can be no doubt. I found arsenic in your father's body after carrying out my tests more than once, and its presence absolutely confirmed my diagnosis at the time of his death. It was not due to natural causes.'

He drew himself up with a little puff of pride.

'I must therefore ask you, sir,' Inspector Redderman added quietly, 'to accompany me to the police office where I shall put certain questions to you.'

It was said. And said briefly and tersely as possible, Miss Unwin thought. No wrapping up of words could now disguise that the police suspicions rested firmly on old Mr Partington's son. On Richard.

On the man for whom she felt – it was only at this instant that she was prepared to acknowledge it to herself – for whom she felt more than she had ever felt for any man, for any human being, in her life before.

Richard, whom she loved surely – Didn't she? Wasn't this what it was? – was being taken to the police office under grave suspicion of being that most reprehensible of murderers, the poisoner. The poisoner of his own father.

But at least he had not behaved like a murderer. In

some deep inside part of her Miss Unwin had feared that the man she had admired, and knew now that she felt love for, at the moment the words had been pronounced that showed he was suspected as a poisoner, would break down, curse, snarl, try to escape, be revealed for what he was.

But, no, instead he simply drew himself up a little as if preparing himself and looked Inspector Redderman straight in the eye.

'Very good,' he said. 'I understand perfectly why you should want to question me, and of course I make no objection to coming with you to the police office.'

Then he was gone. Or rather, Miss Unwin thinking of it all afterwards, realised that in five or ten minutes after those words had been spoken he was gone. He had in fact given her a few instructions about the conduct of the household and a message for the chief clerk at the pin works, and then he had fetched his hat and coat, his new overcoat with the fur collar since the day was chilly for May.

But after those ten minutes he was gone indeed. The house was empty of his presence.

Miss Unwin felt it as if all the furniture, the new furniture that had hardly been there more than a few days, the walnut wood chairs, the velvet ottoman, the tall vases and the rich carpets, as if all had been swept away like dream objects in the cold light of day.

She wanted to sit down where she was in the hall – there was a pair of finely carved benches there now where in old Mr Partington's time there had been not a stick of furniture – and weep. But she shook herself. Richard's commissions had to be carried out first. The girls' lesson had to be picked up again from where it had been interrupted when Richard had asked to see her and the two of them had to be told, without a quiver of voice, that their father had been suddenly called away on business.

So the rest of the day passed. Passed somehow, as if she

86

had been transformed into an automaton and the little clockwork engine inside her had been wound just long enough to keep her going through all the day's usual activities.

But at last the girls were safely in their new white beds with the curtains' pink knots released to hide them from the light.

Then the full reality of what had happened flooded back to her. Richard had been kept at the police office. She had steeled herself to that when he had given her directions which made it clear that it might be several days before he came home again.

But she had allowed herself tiny flickers of hope, little curtain twitches. Perhaps Inspector Redderman would ask Richard only a few questions in his laconic manner and Richard's answers would be so clear, so true, that the Inspector would at once tell him that he was no longer needed. Then he would have come home and life would at once have jumped back to where it had been before.

It had not happened. Her sensible self had known all along that it would not happen. When an old man had died by poison in a household into which few if any others ever penetrated, then that man's sole heir was going to be suspected of the crime however innocent he was. So Richard was suspected and Inspector Redderman was questioning and questioning him, hammering and hammering at him in the hope and expectation that at some moment he would break down and confess to the terrible crime.

That was the way the police worked. Miss Unwin from her days at the very bottom of the social pyramid, her workhouse days when she had lived among the dregs, knew much about the way the police conducted their business.

But now all she wanted to do was weep. She had seen in the old days friends and acquaintances taken away to be questioned by policemen a good deal less well-behaved, a

87

lot more evidently brutal, than Inspector Redderman and she had accepted it as part of life. But now the man who had been taken away was the man she loved.

She forced herself not to let the tears fall.

''Ere, what you looking so down in the dumps about?' It was Vilkins.

She had not even heard her coming, although usually her clumping steps in the old patched black boots she wore could be heard minutes before she appeared.

'Oh, Vilkins. They've taken him, and – and I'm afraid, Vilkins. So afraid.'

Vilkins stood there and looked at her, arms akimbo.

'Thought you was spoony on him,' she said. 'And what's that peeler hauled him off for? That's what I'd like to know.'

So Miss Unwin, plain Unwin once again, told her old friend just why Inspector Redderman had taken Richard to the police office and just why she feared that he might never come back.

'Well,' said Vilkins when her tale was done, 'he didn't do it, did he? Poison the old skinflint?'

'No,' said Unwin.

Just the one single explosion of sound. But somehow it cleared in her mind the last of the tiny niggling suspicion she had had that perhaps, somehow, some impossible how, Richard, her Richard, might have done that impossible thing.

''Course he didn't,' Vilkins said matter-of-factly. 'You wouldn't of got spoony about him if he was that sort. Not you, Unwin.'

'Well, perhaps I might not have done. Perhaps I would somehow have known if that had really been the case.'

'No p'rapses about it. I know you. You wouldn't of done nothing so stupid as that. Not my Unwin.'

Then all that Miss Unwin could do was to sit where she was in the dining room where somehow she had drifted and smile a foolish dazed smile.

For a little Vilkins stood just looking down at her, apron askew as it almost always was, big feet in patched boots sticking out from under her skirt, a drip gradually gathering on the end of her big red dab of a nose.

But then she spoke again.

'Yer. That's all very well, you an' me knowing as how the Master couldn't of done nothing like that. But that ain't a-going to do for that old Inspector Red-what-d'you-call-um, is it?'

'Well, no, my dear, it isn't. It certainly isn't, and that's what I'm afraid of. Suppose no other notion of how old Mr Partington died gets into his head? Suppose he just goes on thinking that Richard was responsible, must be responsible?'

'Yer. That's what he'll do all right.'

But Vilkins' gloom, lugubrious though it was, paradoxically gave Miss Unwin heart. That there was somebody still in the world so true to themselves made her believe, though without a shred of her customary logic, that truth would win in the end.

'But he must be made to see that Richard is not the person responsible,' she said.

'What, old Rediface?'

'Yes. He must be made to see that there could be someone else who did that terrible thing.'

'Well, I dunno. He's a policeman, ain't he?'

'But he's a man too. He has a brain. He can think. Indeed, I rather believe he has more than the ordinary amount of brain, little though I saw of him. And if he has, then if I –'

She stopped.

If I, she had said. And at that moment she had realised that it would be her, that it must be her, who had to put a different notion of what had happened in the house into Inspector Redderman's head. There was no one else who would do it, who would want to do it.

'Yes, Vilkins,' she said on a new note of hopeful

energy, 'If I can manage to persuade him that he must look elsewhere, then – then perhaps Richard will come back to this house, and . . .'

Her voice faded into silence.

'Then there'll be them old wedding bells an' happy ever after,' Vilkins said.

'No,' she said, almost as explosively as when she had decided that Richard Partington could not be the murderer of his own father. 'No, I don't know about that, my dear. That's something too far away to be thought of. No, you must forget that I ever spoke of any such thing, that I even so much as hinted at it.'

'Well, I don't know as 'ow I can do that,' Vilkins answered. 'I mean, you 'ave spoke of it, ain't yer? You 'ave hinted. Well, you done a sight more than hint, if you must know.'

'Yes. Yes, I did, didn't I? But, Vilkins, I was so worried, so distressed. I said things I had not even let myself think before.'

'Not much you didn't,' Vilkins answered. ''Course you did. Any girl would of done. Stands to reason. A nice-looking feller like that, even if he is a bit on the shortish side, a nice-looking feller showing 'ow he felt about you, an' you not know that you felt the same way about 'im. Don't give me that.'

Miss Unwin sighed.

'I suppose you're right really, dear Vilkins,' she said. 'But I promise you I did not let that thought ever take proper shape in my mind, truly I did not.'

'Well, if you says so. Only you must be a sight stronger in the 'ead than what I am. An' in course you are. You must be, or you'd of never got where you are an' left me behind with me broom an' dustpan.'

'Oh, Vilkins, I have not left you behind.'

''Course you 'ave, and so you should. But that's not the trouble just now.'

'No, dear? Then what is?'

'Just that if your Richard didn't done do it, then who did? Who did?'

Chapter Ten

Not for the first time in her life Miss Unwin blessed
Vilkins' common sense. Unerringly, for all that she was
not in any way clever or capable of understanding
anything beyond the most elementary, she had laid her
stubby finger on the crux of the matter.

If Richard Partington had not poisoned his father – and
he had not, he had not – then who had? Because old Mr
Partington had died from the effects of poison. Of arsenic.
Doctor Sumsion's scientific tests had proved that.

So someone must have administered that arsenic.

Administered it – Miss Unwin's brain began to work
again – over a fairly long period. Because the attack that
had in the end carried off the old miser had been no
different from the attacks he had suffered at intervals ever
since her first night in the house and before.

Her thinking mind went step by careful step further
forward. If arsenic had been given to the old man, never
mind for the moment how, it must have been given to him
inside the house or at the pin works. He had never once in
all the weeks she had been in the house moved out of that
limited round. Up in the morning to eat the scanty
breakfast of cheap bread Mrs Meggs provided. More than
half alum in place of flour, she had often said to herself.
Then at once over to the works. There, as she had heard
from Richard, he never moved out of his partitioned-off
sanctum up on the gallery above the clanking and
clattering machines that had over the years made him his
fortune. If anything had to be done outside, it had been
Richard who had been sent, given the exact fare for an

omnibus and sent like an errand boy to do just what he was told.

At midday Mrs Meggs would go hobbling across the yard, every day except Sundays, with a tray on which there was more of her cheap bread and two pieces of hard cheese, a bigger one for old Mr Partington, a smaller for Richard. Then in the evening the old miser would come back to the house to eat the dinner that Mrs Meggs had prepared. Those terrible meagre dinners she herself had endured day after day, made only a little more palatable when Captain Fulcher and his sister had come to dinner.

Captain Fulcher. The name seemed to lie at the logical end of her progression of thought.

There, if anyone, was a person who could have been, not cruel enough, but casually careless enough to have given an old man arsenic. And, after all, had not Richard said that his father had never had any of his attacks before he himself had first visited his Cousin Cornelia and afterwards she, with her brother, had begun to come to dine? Yes, the circumstances certainly told against Captain Fulcher.

But why, why would he have done a thing like that?

'Vilkins,' Miss Unwin said, hoping irrationally for some more help from her friend, 'Vilkins, why would Captain Fulcher – you remember I have told you about him – why would he want to poison old Mr Partington?'

'Don't ask me,' Vilkins replied. 'I ain' no blinking gypsy with her old crystal ball, am I?'

'No. No, I suppose you aren't, my dear. It was just that I hoped you could see what might be in front of your nose when I for the life of me could not.'

'Ain't nothing in front o' my nose, 'cept a drip,' said Vilkins, lifting the back of her hand to deal with that.

'No, but Vilkins, didn't I tell you how each time that Captain Fulcher and his sister came to dine the Captain would bring two bottles of sherry because he so disliked not being offered any wine? Well, he could have put

94

arsenic into one of those before it ever entered the house.'

'He could of, yes,' Vilkins agreed solemnly. 'Didn't you tell me as 'ow he always opened both the bottles at once, soon as ever he got 'ere? I thought that was funny at the time. He could of saved one bottle, 'case the first wasn't all drunk.'

'Yes,' Miss Unwin chimed in. 'When I saw him do that I thought it was no more than a reflection of his nature, that he was the sort of man who never did anything by halves, who never looked ahead and counted the costs.'

'Terrible gambler, you did say.'

'Yes, he was on the very point once, after a money-lender called Mr Davis came forcing his way into the house, of asking old Mr Partington for a loan. Only he realised that there was no chance ever of that.'

'An' 'im with all them sovereigns under the flags.'

Miss Unwin almost gasped then. She stood rapt for a moment, hands clasped in an attitude not far from prayer. Grateful prayer.

'Vilkins,' she said at last, 'you've done it again, put your finger on the very thing.'

''ave I? Well, that's a miracle.'

'Vilkins, Captain Fulcher knew about Mr Partington's gold, I'm almost sure of that. He learnt of it from the girls. They would chatter and tease him and, though once when I heard them I did not realise that they might have told him anything they shouldn't, later I did suspect it. I realised it when I was telling old Mr Partington that the girls knew where some of his hoard was hidden. I thought of Captain Fulcher for a moment then, but I didn't dare tell Mr Partington his secret was known to a man like that. And then in all the troubles afterwards I forgot.'

'Yer, that's all very well, Unwin. But I can't see what you're so excited about, 'opping up an' down like you got fleas.'

'But don't you see, my dear? Don't you see? If Captain Fulcher knew about that gold, wasn't he almost bound to

95

try to get hold of some of it? He was being dunned, and then, without him mentioning that he had won money at the races or anything of that kind, suddenly he no longer spoke of being in difficulties. He must surely have got hold of enough of Mr Partington's hidden wealth to stave off his creditors.'

'Well, what if he did? Ain't no reason to murder the poor old man, is it?'

'Not unless he wished at all costs to prevent Mr Partington discovering he had been robbed and, as he was bound to do, suspecting anyone with access to the house. Not unless that.'

''Ere,' Vilkins said, 'you may be right.'

Miss Unwin drew herself up.

'Yes, I may be right,' she said. 'Or I may not be. But one thing is certain. I have remembered facts and circumstances which Inspector Redderman is quite unaware of. And I must see that he gets to know of them at once.'

'An' 'ow are you a-going to do that?'

'Why, quite simply. I am going to tell him.'

She set off for the police office almost immediately. There was nothing to keep her. The twins were safely in their beds and Vilkins was there to make sure they stayed where they had been put.

On the steps of the police station, not so far along the Harrow Road, she did hesitate for a moment.

What if Inspector Redderman was not there? What if he had callously left Richard to wait in some cell while he went home to the comforts of his own hearth? But as soon as she had thought of it she rejected the notion. If the Inspector was at all the man she had found him to be, brief though her acquaintance with him was, then he was not one to waste time. He would use every minute during which he had Richard at his disposal to question him. He would use each minute to the last second.

Miss Unwin mounted the police station steps, pushed

open its heavy door, presented herself at a mahogany counter where a portly sergeant sat overflowing a high stool.

'Inspector Redderman?' he said in answer to her inquiry. 'And what would you be wanting with the Inspector, my dear? That is, madam. Madam.'

A little belatedly he had realised that the slight upright figure in front of him, despite the plainness of her attire, was not an upper servant or a shopkeeper's wife to be addressed in the familiar manner but a lady, to whom respect was due and must be paid.

'It is in connection with his inquiries into the decease of the late Mr Partington,' Miss Unwin replied sedately.

But her words plainly gave the bulky sergeant cause for alarm.

'Mr Partington, Mr Partington,' he said. 'I think perhaps the Inspector will be very pleased to see you.'

He gave a vigorous thump to the domed handbell on the counter beside him. A constable appeared with a clatter of heavy boots, and Miss Unwin was led speedily to an office deep inside the building.

And there sitting on either side of a plain wooden table were Inspector Redderman and Richard Partington.

Richard, Miss Unwin saw as soon as she set foot in the room, was looking far from his usual self. His round face was lined and almost haggard. His shoulders drooped. The fine new clothes he had bought himself so recently looked somehow less fine.

Oh, that I should notice all this so instantly, Miss Unwin thought. Yes, if I did not know it before, I know it now. There, sitting bedraggled in front of a police inspector and in danger of the gallows, is the man I love.

Inspector Redderman bobbed neatly up in his chair. He, Miss Unwin, saw, did not look a whit different from the person she had met that morning, spare, controlled, within himself.

She wondered suddenly whether she had after all done

97

the right thing in coming hurrying round to him with her information.

But, she reassured herself firmly, it was information that she had to give him and information that he ought to have.

'Turner,' Inspector Redderman said to the constable, 'take this gentleman downstairs.'

Richard at once pulled himself to his feet. Miss Unwin was aware that he was obeying an order, though the Inspector had said nothing to him directly, and she hated to think that the Richard Partington who had been her employer was now a man who was given orders and obeyed them without a sign of protest. The hours he had been in the police office had taken more out of him than she would have believed possible of the person who had endured his father's jibes and deprivations so long and so uncomplainingly.

The constable closed the door behind his charge.

'Miss Unwin?' Inspector Redderman said.

Miss Unwin swallowed.

'Inspector, I have brought you certain information which I think may be relevant to your inquiries.'

'Sit down, Miss.'

Miss Unwin took the chair Richard had just vacated. With a shock of recognition she was aware of the lingering heat of his body on the hard surface of the wood beneath her.

She felt herself lose colour.

But the Inspector did not seem to notice her discomposure.

'Now,' he said, 'tell me.'

So Miss Unwin produced her story of the finding of the gold, of the twins' silly behaviour, of the extraordinary visit from the plump and assertive Mr Davis and of what she thought Captain Fulcher must know.

The Inspector listened without moving a muscle, without a flicker of his quiet grey eyes.

98

At last Miss Unwin came to a halt. She was conscious, angrily conscious, that she had told her tale with less than her usual clarity.

'I see,' the Inspector said. 'And you have nothing more you wish to tell me?'

'No, No, I do not think so. But – But you must see . . .'

She faltered to a stop. How could she tell this man who seemed to know so well just exactly what he was doing what it was that he ought to infer from the account she had given him?

Inspector Redderman half-rose from his chair on the other side of the table with its squared-off piles of paper, its inkpot with the lid meticulously closed, its blotter neatly aligned.

'Then I will bid you good evening,' he said.

'But – But are you not going to take any action arising from what I have told you? Are you not going to say that Rich– that Mr Partington may return home?'

'No, Miss.'

For a moment Miss Unwin was ready to accept the two brief words of dismissal. They seemed so definite.

But a dart of rebelliousness leapt up.

'But why? Why, Inspector?' she cried.

'Because you have given me little more than a tangle of suppositions,' the Inspector answered quietly. 'Until such facts as there are have been verified I can see no reason for any action.'

It was like a douche of cold water. But Miss Unwin recognised that the water was the plain water of truth. What she had told the Inspector was indeed largely supposition, though she believed it was logical supposition. And the facts that it rested on ought, of course, to be verified before any responsible person acted upon them. But nonetheless the douche was chilling.

'Very well, Inspector,' she said, 'I will return home now, and expect to see you tomorrow if you should wish to talk to the twins.'

'Yes, I may need to do that.'

And that was her dismissal.

Wearily she trod her way back along the Harrow Road, her steps a great deal slower and heavier than when she had made the journey in the other direction.

It was only as she reached out to the house's doorbell to summon Vilkins to open for her that she made up her mind.

What she had told Inspector Redderman might be only supposition. But there was a good chance, more than a good chance, that she was right and that it had indeed been Captain Fulcher who had given old Mr Partington arsenic in order to prevent him finding out that some of his gold hoard had gone. Of course, to anyone convinced that the murder must have been the work of the old miser's direct heir this alternative account might seem flimsy enough. But she herself knew that Richard Partington was not to blame for his father's death.

She knew it. She knew it.

So it was all the more likely that Captain Fulcher was responsible. However few confirmed facts there were to base that supposition on.

But other facts there must be that supported it. And, waiting in the faint chill of the early May evening for Vilkins to come to the door, Miss Unwin made up her mind that she herself would go and find whatever more facts there were that could be found.

She owed Richard that. She owed that to the man who had in moments of distress called the governess he employed by her forename. Harriet owed that to Richard.

As soon as Vilkins had pulled the heavy front door open she told her what had been the result of her visit to the police office and what she had now determined to do.

'What you want to get a-hold of,' said Vilkins, 'is the feller's betting book.'

'Betting book?' Miss Unwin asked, less worldly-wise in certain matters than her friend.

100

'Yer. Don't you know? Gentlemen in the racing world always has 'em. Betting books. They writes down what money they's lost an' the name o' the 'orses what they lost it on. Puts down what they won, too, I s'pose.'

'Yes, yes, I see. If Captain Fulcher's betting book shows that he was much in debt and then was able to pay off those sums without having won anything at the races, then I shall have a fact indeed to take back to Inspector Redderman.'

'Only, 'ow you going to get 'old of the book?' Vilkins said.

'I shall go to the Captain's lodgings,' Miss Unwin answered at once. 'I know where they are, just off Oxford Street. I heard old Mr Partington abusing him once for having an expensive address and the Captain replying that a fellow must live somewhere where the wretched tradesmen will suppose he has money. So I shall go there tomorrow and trust that I can persuade someone to let me in. I shall choose a time when the Captain is likely to be out, and his sister of course will have gone back to the country now. She dislikes London and its flies and foul air so much.'

Miss Unwin had calculated that she would have to wait until the evening to be sure that Captain Fulcher would not be at his lodgings. She thought with dismay that this would mean that Richard would in all likelihood have to spend all the next day still at the police station. But she had reckoned without Vilkins' knowledge of the low side of life.

'He won't be at 'ome today,' she said when early in the morning Miss Unwin told her of her plan. 'There's the fight today. He'll 'ave been off over Reading way crack o'dawn. Feller like 'im ain't going to miss the chance o' losing a good bet, not when it's Jem Falkinder against the Black Mauler.'

'A boxing match, Vilkins? But how do you know about that?'

101

'Well, I talks, don't I? The chap what buys the rabbit skins off of us, that's who told me.'

'So if I can give the twins something to do which will keep them occupied this morning, I can go to his lodgings and perhaps be back before midday.'

Miss Unwin's heart leapt up. Secretly she added to herself, *be back before midday with evidence that even Inspector Redderman must take notice of*.

And then Richard will come home again, she thought. And the nightmare will be no more than that, a dream to be forgotten in the broad daylight.

The hope buoyed her up all the way to the West End respectability of Great Marlborough Street and Captain Fulcher's lodgings. She was unable in advance to think of how she would penetrate the Captain's rooms but she had no doubt she would easily enough overcome any obstacle a landlady might constitute.

Her optimism proved altogether justified.

She rang at the bell. Almost at once the door was opened by a slatternly girl of thirteen or fourteen in a dirty apron. A broom was propped against the wall just behind her.

'There's no one at 'ome but me,' she said without waiting to see what this visitor wanted.

Miss Unwin summed her up at once.

'That's perfectly all right,' she said clearly and loudly. 'I have come to give something to Captain Fulcher, if you will just show me up to his room I will write a note and explain.'

'Oh, yes, mum,' said the girl.

She turned and trailed off along the hall passageway and up the stairs to the first floor.

'It's there,' she said, indicating the nearest door with a jerk of her head.

'Good. Thank you,' Miss Unwin said, still vigorously determined.

The wretched girl slouched off back to her broom. Miss

Unwin took the doorknob of the Captain's rooms firmly in her hand and turned it.

In her mind's eye she saw the betting book she so much needed as lying immediately before her on some convenient table. She told herself not to be ridiculous. In all likelihood a thorough search would be necessary. Drawers would have to be pried into. Cupboards opened. This was not the sort of behaviour she saw of herself. But the case was urgent and she was not going to be halted now by considerations of what was ladylike and proper.

The sitting room that confronted her was much as she had expected. Its furniture was not really shabby but none of it was of a piece. The sofa was too feminine for a person of Captain Fulcher's taste and neither of the chairs, though they were good enough, matched it quite in colour. There was a table. But on it no sign of a book, only two or three newspapers evidently at least of the day before, crumpled and carelessly tossed down. There was an escritoire, however, and its topmost drawer was even invitingly half an inch open.

Next to it was an inner door which, Miss Unwin thought, must lead to the Captain's bedroom. She wondered whether she ought to glance in there before she tackled the likely escritoire.

But she had no time to decide. The door she was looking at abruptly swept open and standing in the doorway wearing a green silk wrapper and with no front of false hair under the cap on her head was none other than Cousin Cornelia.

Chapter Eleven

Miss Unwin's mind went blank. The appearance so abruptly of someone she had thought safely down in Somerset, here in a place where she herself was about to commit a criminal act, however good her intentions, robbed her of all thought.

She stood staring at the apparition of Cousin Cornelia. And Cousin Cornelia indeed was something to stare at. Never at the best of times with her thin knife of a nose and her stringy neck anything of a beauty, caught now without the elaborate toilettes she affected on her visits of ceremony to the Harrow Road, she looked like nothing so much as a scarecrow. Deprived of her gowns of bottle-green or cherry-red silks, of her lace shawls and her caps of yet more delicate lace, she was revealed as the old-before-her-time creature that she really was.

Miss Unwin, when thought from some far banished place began to roll back into her mind, found herself wondering that she had even recognised this elderly apparition as Captain Fulcher's devoted sister.

But, if she had almost failed to recognise Miss Fulcher, Miss Fulcher, it now appeared, had completely failed to recognise her.

'Pray, who are you?' she demanded. 'What are you doing in my rooms? I thought you were that servant girl.'

Evidently in her visits to the man she hoped to marry, Cousin Cornelia had taken so little notice of his children's governess that, bonneted and in a mantle now, she had not remembered her in the least.

Miss Unwin, mistress of herself again, was quick to take

advantage of this piece of unforeseen luck.

'Madam,' she said rapidly, 'my humblest apologies. I must have mistaken the door.'

At once she turned and hurried back across the room. Cousin Cornelia said nothing. No doubt the intrusion, unexpected as it was, had considerably discomposed her. Miss Unwin seized the doorknob, turned it.

And as she did so, she saw on a small console table up against the wall beside the door, which she had not noticed on entering, a pair of Captain Fulcher's gloves with beside them a little black leather-bound book. From its scuffed appearance and a trace of yellow mud running across it, it looked like an object frequently taken out-of-doors. Captain Fulcher's betting book. It could be nothing else.

Could she put out a hand and snatch it up? But, no, although she could not see Miss Fulcher, and indeed did not dare turn and give her another opportunity of observing her features, she knew almost for certain that that lady must be looking at her with surprised intent. No, there was no way in which she could pluck up the little scuffed black book she needed so much to peruse.

So near and yet so far.

Hastily she stepped out on to the landing, pulling the door of the rooms firmly closed behind her. Quickly she made for the stairs and went down them.

If suddenly Cousin Cornelia felt she did after all know this intruder, she might easily come out and call to her. Only in the street would it be really safe, since the lady happily was by no means dressed to show herself to the world.

But at the open house-door the down-at-heel little servant girl was standing looking out at the passing scene, leaning on her broom and scratching with skirt half-uplifted at a dirty knee.

Miss Unwin felt a sharp flame of fury. Why hadn't the

106

creature told her that Miss Fulcher was in the Captain's rooms? Had it not been for Cousin Cornelia's inability to recognise a person from a lower social sphere out of her correct place, she herself would have been caught in a situation she would have found it impossible to extricate herself from without a humiliating confession.

'Why, you wretch,' she exclaimed, before more reasonable thoughts intervened. 'You never told me Captain Fulcher's sister was there. Why not? What possessed you?'

'Forgot, Miss,' said the girl, bursting into tears.

Or rather, Miss Unwin thought not without a certain remaining fury, she trickled into tears, sniffing and sobbing in a manner more repulsive than pathetic.

'Stop that,' she said to her. 'Stop it at once.'

The poor creature gave one last sucking sniff and stopped it.

And it occurred then to Miss Unwin that while she had her thus under her thumb there might be information to be got out of her.

'Tell me,' she said, without preliminary or excuse, 'does Captain Fulcher pay his bills?'

'That he don't, Miss, that he don't.'

'But he did pay them some little time ago? Didn't he pay off what he owed a little while ago?'

Perhaps this evidence would be as good as that in the untouchable, unseeable betting book. If the girl knew that the Captain had suddenly become flush with money, as she was likely enough to have gathered from her employer, then she could in her turn tell Inspector Redderman, or her employer could tell him with yet more authority. Then the Inspector would see that the 'supposition' which had been put to him by Richard Partington's governess was more substantial than he had chosen to credit. Then he would see that the case against Richard Partington, which he evidently thought so

107

obvious, was not as firm as he believed. And then perhaps he would begin to see the justice of releasing Richard from his endless questioning.

'Oh, no, Miss,' the snivelling girl said. 'The Capting ain't hardly never paid what he owes. Me mistress says he'll 'ave to go. She's said it a thousand times. But she can't shift 'im. He stays an' he stays.'

'What is this? You must have misunderstood. I tell you, not so long ago Captain Fulcher was suddenly well in funds. He must have paid off something at least.'

'No, 'e did not, Miss. An' I'm the one what's likely to know. I'm the one, ain't I, what hears the mistress telling an' telling the master to get 'im out, an' the master makin' excuses 'cos he gets tips off of 'im for the hosses.'

Miss Unwin felt her rage, and her hopes, slowly sink.

'You're quite, quite sure of all this?' she asked.

But she knew even as she spoke that the girl could hardly be mistaken.

'Oh, yes, Miss. I knows all about 'im, I do. I got ears in me 'ead, ain't I? An' if gennelmen will talk an' rant in their loud voices, I'm going to 'ear, ain't I?'

'Yes, I suppose you are.'

Miss Unwin, somewhere in the well-behaved part of her mind, thought she ought to rebuke this little eavesdropper. But she lacked the heart to do it.

'Yes,' the girl went on, in a voice that whined unpleasantly from one single note to another. 'Yes, the Captain's sister 'as gone an' give 'im every penny what she's got. Rented off a big 'ouse what was leff 'er in a Will she did, to give 'im money for 'is betting an' 'is gaming. Which is why she lives 'ere and complains about us every day of 'er life. An' he's 'ad every pound of her 'heritance. That I do know. But she don't blame 'im for it. Not never. Oh, Jack, she says, what terrible, terrible luck you do 'ave.'

But now Miss Unwin's conscience was aroused.

'Listen to me, my girl,' she said. 'You have no business

to tittle-tattle about your betters like that. If ever I hear of you doing it again, I shall tell your mistress.'

But the awful girl just put out her tongue then.

'An' she'd tell the master to take a stick to me,' she said. 'An' he'd never do nothing about it, 'cos he's too lazy to move hisself.'

Miss Unwin lifted her head at that and swept off down the street.

But her renewed spasm of rage scarcely lasted till she had reached the nearest corner. It was replaced by sweeping feelings of doubt.

Captain Fulcher had not, it seemed almost certain, had that sudden access of funds which would have resulted from his discovery of one of old Mr Partington's gold hoards. So it was probable indeed that he had not stolen from the old miser, that he was not in fear of the theft being discovered and attributed to him. So, then, he had no reason to take the old man's life.

And now, Miss Unwin thought, as she mounted the steep steps of a brightly placarded omnibus, there is no one whom I can propose to Inspector Redderman as a more likely murderer than Richard. My Richard.

The very idea suffocated rational thought in her head. The rest of her journey home, the change from one omnibus to a second, the congested traffic in the streets round her, the shouts and yells of the drivers, the neighings of their horses, the crack of carters' whips, the shouting of newsboys with their bundles of midday editions, all passed by her in a blur of unthinking misery.

Her state of anaesthetised nothingness persisted when she reached the house. The twins needed attention. They had abandoned the tasks they had been set, and Vilkins had not been able to persuade them to go back to them.

But Miss Unwin knew she had dealt with them mechanically. Indeed, next day she could not remember what punishment task she had given them, though she was pleased to find she had retained in her misery enough authority to have made them carry it out.

It was not until the evening even that she had spirit enough to tell her confederate what had happened on her visit to Captain Fulcher's rooms and the sad conclusion she had been forced to draw.

'Yerss, you're right,' Vilkins said in a voice reeking with gloom. 'That old Captain ain't the one. You can be sure o' that.'

'Oh, sure of it I am,' Miss Unwin replied, hardly less depressed. 'But what I am not sure of at all is, if Captain Fulcher is not the person who administered that arsenic, then who is? It can't be Richard. It cannot be.'

'If you says so, Unwin. If you says so.'

'Then who can it be? It must have been someone in the house, if not living here then a visitor. Old Mr Partington never went out and when he was over at the pin works he never ate except what Mrs Meggs took across to him.'

'I reckon she must be the one then,' Vilkins said. 'Pity I never saw 'er. I could of told then. One look at 'er an ' I could of told.'

Miss Unwin smiled.

'Oh, she may be the person we're looking for,' she said. 'In logic she could be. But only as much as anyone else in the house, myself, Richard, the twins even. But, I cannot go to Inspector Redderman again after he has derided what I told him before unless I take with me a piece of evidence even he cannot ignore.'

'What's evidence?' Vilkins asked.

'Oh, my dear, it's a fact so strong that it cannot be gainsaid. Something like that is what I need at this moment.'

'Well, that old Meggs is your best 'ope, far as I can see.'

'Yet she liked old Mr Partington, Vilkins. If ever she did anyone a good turn it was him. He was the one who got a helping at dinner that was more than barely enough to keep body and soul together. He was the one who got the big teacup in the evenings. No, Mrs Meggs for some reason or another had a soft spot for that old miser. You remember I told you what a demon she was when I showed Richard where that gold was hidden?'

'Yerss. Spiteful old witch. Wish I could get a good look at 'er.'

It was then that an idea came to Miss Unwin, and with it revivified hope.

'Yes,' she said. 'Yes, yes.'

'Yes, what? You gone off your 'ead or something?'

'Yes, you shall get a look at Mrs Meggs, my dear. Not that I expect you to see anything that provides convincing proof –'

'I might,' Vilkins said. 'Don't see why I shouldn't. I got eyes in me 'ead, ain't I?'

'Yes, yes, my dear, you have. And I would not be at all surprised if you did see something that would help. But that's not what I have most in mind.'

'Well, what do you 'ave then?'

'That she must be questioned. It is plain that the police have no intention of even going near her. Inspector Redderman is going to go on and on questioning Richard, and can think of nothing else. In a way I scarcely blame him. It's his nearest road to a solution.'

'Yeh. But the nearest road ain't always the best.'

'No. No, you're right. So what I propose is that we two go somehow and see Mrs Meggs. That we put questions to her in the same way that Inspector Redderman is putting questions to Richard.'

'Well, it'll 'ave to be you as does that, Unwin. I don't know one question from another.'

'Well, perhaps it would be best. But I shall have your eyes with me, Vilkins dear. And they may be what brings us to a good end at the last.'

'Yer. Well, where's she gone then, this Mrs Meggs o' yours?'

Miss Unwin's heart plummeted.

'Vilkins, I don't know,' she said.

Indeed, the old housekeeper had left so abruptly and in such a rage that there had been no question of asking her where she was going, and she had done nothing about reclaiming such possessions as she had left behind.

'Vilkins, what shall I do?' Miss Unwin went on, sounding for once plaintive and feebly feminine.

'I could ask that old rabbit-skin man,' Vilkins said. 'He was telling me the day before yesterday 'ow he used to call 'ere regular, even though he got a skin only once in a blue moon. And then the old skinflint wanted a penny more for it than any other customer. But he talked to 'er all right, and he could of 'eard something about 'er that'd tell us where to look. He's a regular chatterbox, that one. Not that I mind, in course.'

So Miss Unwin had to be patient. Patience was something she usually found within her grasp, even though her nature urged her always to find out anything she wanted to know as soon as she could. Now, however, she discovered that self-imposed patience was another thing that had deserted her when the dazzlement of love had so unexpectedly invaded her inner world.

The rabbit-skin man called only twice a week. So it could not be until the afternoon of the next day that there would be the least hope of learning where old Mrs Meggs had gone. But during the night – Miss Unwin slept little and restlessly – one other way forward did come into her mind. If old Mr Partington had been poisoned, she thought, then it would be as well to find out as much as she could about the arsenic that had killed him. Then when she came to tackle the old housekeeper, if she ever did, she would be in a better position to put a question that might make her betray herself without realising it.

So in the morning, as soon as the shops in the West End would be open, she once more set the poor twins an exercise to do, promising herself that when Richard was back she would make up in extra zeal for all the time of hers they had lost. Then she put on bonnet, gloves and mantle and stepped boldly out. She was lucky in seeing a cab, a four-wheeler, slowly making its way along the road without a fare. She hailed it.

'Oxford Street,' she said. 'Stop at the largest bookshop you see.'

And there in the bookshop she asked for a volume on poisons. The assistant could not refrain from giving her a look of intense curiosity.

Spiritedly she invented.

'My father is Professor Unwin,' she said. 'He requires a comprehensive volume immediately.'

'Yes, madam, of course. I believe we have just the article.'

The assistant hurried away and returned in a very few minutes with a large book. Miss Unwin looked at the title. *Potherton on Poisons*.

'I think my father will find that just what he requires,' she said.

It was all she could do to wait while the assistant wrapped her purchase in brown paper and neatly tied it with a loop of string for her to carry it by. In the cab, a hansom, in which she returned she tore off the paper and eagerly turned to the stout volume's index. There was a satisfying number of entries under 'Arsenic'.

But, she said to herself, as with the book again open in front of her, she supervised the rest of the twins' morning lessons, learning about arsenic will be only half the battle. It is finding Mrs Meggs that is the first task, and for that I have to wait upon the whim of a wretched rabbit-skin chatterbox.

At last, however, when Miss Unwin returned with the girls from their afternoon walk, Vilkins, who had opened the front door for them, whispered in a frank shower of spit into her ear.

'He's been. I'll tell you.'

'Go up to your room, girls, and take off your hats and cloaks,' Miss Unwin said.

'Can't we take them off here and Mary go up with them?' said Louisa. 'It's a fag going all the way up and then having to come all the way down again.'

'And it's a task which teaches you that everything in this world is not easy. Off you go.'

Louisa went, with Maria obediently behind her.

'Yes?' said Miss Unwin, almost before the two of them were out of hearing.

'Well, it ain't so good.'

Miss Unwin felt a dart of rage. She had, somehow, counted on Vilkins getting exactly what they needed to know out of the rabbit-skin man and she had been let down.

'What do you mean it's not so good?'

''E don't know.'

'But you said he would.'

'Only thought 'e would, didn't I? Thought a chatterbox like 'im would be bound to 'ave learnt where she come from, or if she 'ad relations anywhere about, something like that.'

'And he knew nothing?'

'Didn't know much, that's for sure.'

'But he knew something. What was it? What was it?'

'Well, all he really said was the old witch told 'im once what she wanted to do when she'd finished 'ere.'

'And what was that? Does it help? Oh, Vilkins, tell me.'

'Don't see as 'ow it does 'elp, not a bit.'

'But what, Vilkins, what?'

'Wanted to set up in a public 'ouse. Never hadn't had no liquor most of 'er life, wanted to 'ave a pub of her own. An' drink all the cellar, I dare say.'

'And did she tell the man where she intended to set up in this public house?'

114

'No. Never said nothing about that. He said as 'ow she told 'im once she didn't think the old feller was a-going to die for many a long day, an' as 'ow she'd 'ave to wait an' wait till 'e did afore she got what he'd left 'er in 'is Will an' she could put it with 'er bit o' savings.'

'Vilkins,' said Miss Unwin, with dawning delight. 'You see what this means?'

'Can't say as I do, no. Not really.'

'It means she wanted him to die. It means that, though she was loyal to him, nevertheless she wanted him to die before her. She wanted him to die so that she could set up her public house somewhere and have time to enjoy it.'

'Well, if she did she's got it now. But we ain't got no idea where she 'as got it. Nor any 'ope of finding out, if you ask me.'

'Yes. Yes, I'm afraid you're right.'

Miss Unwin felt her brief flame of excitement die away.

'She could be anywhere in the whole country,' she said. 'One wretched public house. How are we to find it?'

'Dunno,' said Vilkins.

It took Miss Unwin till late that night, very late, to hit on the answer.

She had settled herself again to a study of the weighty *Potherton on Poisons*. Hour upon hour she had read, turning from one arsenic reference to another. She learnt of the powder's uses in industry and commerce, of its supposed properties in heightening the female complexion, of its medical uses, of mispickel, realgar and orpiment, of Fowler's Solution and the Durkheim springs.

And suddenly while she was in the middle of an abstruse passage on severe gastro-enteritis, in which she recognised more or less the symptoms she had seen in Mr Partington, the answer to her other problem arrived in her mind.

Simple. If Mrs Meggs had bought a public house she

would have had to get hold of a going business or to have obtained equipment for a new one. And, again, she would have had to become a new customer at a brewery. One of these activities could, surely, be traced through a commercial agency. It might take time. It would certainly take money. But it could be done. If it was going to save Richard, it must be done.

In the event it proved startlingly easy. Next day had perforce to be another dull morning for Louisa and Maria. She set them pages of the copy book to write out. Then, once again she took a cab, but this time to the City. There, without much inquiry, she located a firm of agents who, with never a question asked but with several sovereigns from her rapidly diminishing savings passed over, undertook to make the necessary inquiries.

She felt as if she was living a fairy story when the very next morning there was a letter addressed to her and in it she read, in a clerk's regular copperplate hand, that a Mrs Susan Meggs had started a business as a public house at 14 Nile Street, London E. *Nile Street*, the helpful firm added, *is to be found off the Ratcliff Highway.*

'The Ratcliff 'ighway,' Vilkins said, when she told her the good news. 'That's bad.'

Chapter Twelve

Miss Unwin realised as soon as Vilkins had made her downright comment that the fact that Mrs Meggs's new public house was situated off the Ratcliff Highway was indeed not good news. The Ratcliff Highway was notorious. Running beside the ever-busy Docks, seamen of every nationality and race thronged it with, if all that she had heard was true, the women who catered for men paid off after long voyages ready and willing for a spree. Robbery was a daily, or rather nightly, occurrence. Fights were frequent and bloody. And, above all, no female who was not of the lowest sort was considered to be safe there.

But Mrs Meggs must be seen, Ratcliff Highway or no Ratcliff Highway.

There was another, different difficulty, too, about herself and Vilkins setting out for this dangerous locality. Richard Partington's daughters were, after all, now her responsibility. She should not leave them in the house for any considerable period with only the newly arrived cook, Mrs Miller, to look after them. Louisa certainly could almost be counted on to take advantage of such a situation to launch out on some escapade or other. It was in her nature. And her twin, though less of a madcap, would always follow. Their discovery of their grandfather's gold was proof enough of that.

So the only course open to her was to venture down the Ratcliff Highway after dark, when the girls were safely asleep. But this would mean that she and Vilkins would arrive at the Docks at the worst time possible. By day most of the area's inhabitants would be busily at work. At night they would be on the loose, prowling like tigers.

Yet there seemed no other possible course. If some evidence was to be found to show that Richard Partington was not the only person who was likely to have murdered his father, then to Dockland by night they must go.

Some precautions, however, Miss Unwin was able to take. She asked Vilkins if she might borrow from her some garments that did not proclaim her at once a lady.

'In course you shall 'ave what you want,' Vilkins declared. ''Cept my bonnet. I must keep that for meself, it's so fine.'

Miss Unwin remembered Vilkins' bonnet then. It was 'fine', a big straw which even without the wide red ribbon sewn round it was famously conspicuous.

'Oh, Vilkins dear,' she said, 'do you think you ought to wear a bonnet like that in a place like the Ratcliff Highway?'

'An' why not, I should like to know.'

'Well, my dear, I hardly like to say this. It is a fine bonnet, I know, and you looked well in it in Bayswater on your evenings out, as I recall. But . . . But in another part of the city, a part where . . . Well, where there are girls who . . .'

''Ere, I know what you're a-trying to say. That I'd look like a dollymop. That's it, isn't it?'

'Well, dear, it is a bonnet that people will look at.'

'An' so it should be. If you're a-going down Ratcliff 'Ighway, Unwin, it'd be as well you too looked like most o' the girls we'll see. An' don't you be thinking nothing else.'

Miss Unwin paused and reflected.

'Yes, Vilkins dear, you are perfectly right. I do not know that nowadays I could carry myself that way with any assurance. I have learnt so long to be respectable. But if you feel that you can do it, then perhaps it would after all give us a measure of protection. Only . . .'

'Only you don't want me to go and pick up trade, eh? Don't you worry. I knows 'ow to scare 'em off, just as well as I knows 'ow to make 'em look.'

'Then so be it, my dear.'

''Ere, but there's something else we ought to take.'

'Yes? What's that? I rely on you, dear. You have had experience of that world, the world beneath as I call it, more recently than I.'

'So I 'ave. An' lucky for you it is.'

'Then what else do you recommend we take?'

'Knives,' said Vilkins. 'A pair o' knives from out o' the kitchen drawer.'

So it was with a knife each hidden in their pockets that Miss Unwin and Vilkins approached the Ratcliff Highway that evening. Vilkins, Miss Unwin had to concede, looked in her garish bonnet every inch a street-walker, but one well capable of looking after herself. In Vilkins' second skirt herself, and with an old mantle of her own scissor-shorn of its decoration, she hoped she made a reasonable companion to her friend, somewhat more respectable but by no means looking the lady.

The scene in front of them as they entered the wide road certainly made their precautions seem necessary. It was as lively as any daytime street further west in the primmer parts of the great metropolis. Men of every colour and creed in the wide world, it seemed, strolled and rollicked along both pavements and roadway. There were Chinese and Negroes, lithe brown-skinned Malays, white-turbanned lascars, great hulking fair-haired Swedes and Norwegians, bold red-shirted Americans, their twanging speech loudly out-topping all the noise around them.

For a moment the governess in Miss Unwin came to the surface. What a lesson in geography lay before her. How strikingly could she demonstrate to her pupils the variety of humankind from the throng that sauntered and eddied by. But no such lesson could ever be. Because, besides the

119

seamen from so many lands and the lightermen and ballast-heavers and coal-heavers from the area itself, there were the women of the Highway.

They put Vilkins and her gaudy bonnet to shame. Few of them, indeed, wore anything on their heads at all. Instead long greasy locks tossed in the light of the lamps and the harsh glare coming from the raw gas-jets outside the many shops vying still for business. Bright shawls, brilliant red, vivid green, blatant blue, dazzled the eye over blouses often torn or mud-streaked and always so low-cut as to be open invitations. Brass heels on red shoes trod through the black and greasy puddles of the roadway or clattered on its dark cobbles.

'Vilkins,' Miss Unwin said, 'who are we to ask where Nile Street is to be found? We cannot approach creatures like those.'

'We could. If we 'ad to. You can talk to anyone an' 'ope they'll listen. But we can do better nor that.'

And Vilkins, whose eyes had been darting hither and thither over the noisy scene, suddenly moved forward and pounced.

Her quarry was a hot-eel boy, a dirty ragged creature of nine or ten with a broken-wheeled cart on which rested his brazier and the slices of eel he was frying.

'Eels, all 'ot, eels all 'ot. Ha'penny a piece. Come an' get 'em. Come an' get 'em.'

'We'll 'ave a couple o' them,' Vilkins said, taking a penny from her purse careful not to show its contents too broadly, small though they were.

The boy handed them each a piece of white-fleshed, strong-smelling eel, smoking slightly, on a pair of scratched and battered tin plates.

''Ere, this is good,' Vilkins said, sinking her teeth in.

Miss Unwin followed her example, telling herself firmly that in her youngest days she would have been overjoyed to get anything as tasty and solid to eat. But she found those days were far away, and eel as badly cooked as it had

120

been by the ragged urchin in front of them not at all to her taste.

Yet she made herself eat and smile. She knew what Vilkins had come to the boy for.

At last Vilkins handed back her little platter with only the centre bone of her piece of eel left on it.

'Can you tell me where Nile Street is?' she said.

The boy looked at her in astonishment.

'What,' he said, his voice loud even among all the surrounding noise, 'yer don't know Nile Street? Where you come from then?'

Would he expose them as a pair of intruders? Would he draw the attention of anyone looking for prey?

Miss Unwin cast a nervous glance round.

'Yeh,' Vilkins answered the boy, her voice even louder. 'We been away, see. Guests of 'Er Majesty. Long-stay guests, too, weren't we, dear?'

Miss Unwin nearly missed her cue. But from somewhere in her long ago past she brought up the answer, and in her voice of old.

'Too bloody long,' she said. 'Too bloody long by far.'

'What you get sent down for then?' the urchin asked. 'You two in a bawdy-house, was yer?'

'You mind your business, 'less you want a clip round the ear. An' where is Nile Street, if you're so clever?'

'All right, all right. Up on the right. Past Paddy's Goose.'

Vilkins linked her arm through Miss Unwin's and moved off.

'Paddy's Goose,' she said, 'know what that is? I've 'eard talk about it.'

'No. No, I've no idea what it is. What is it?'

'It's a public house. Not the one we're looking for, in course. It's a big, big place. Does a roaring trade if what I heard's true. Got the name they call it by from the sign. It's the White Swan truly.'

'Well, I wish we were past it and in Nile Street.'

Certainly Miss Unwin had cause to wish the expedition at least half-way over. The crowds were getting rowdier by the minute. Groups were standing in three parts drunken circles singing.

'Oh, Mexico was covered in snow, the grub was bad and the pay was low,' was the one set of words she was at all able to make out.

Other groups were gyrating in clod-hopping dances. There was one thumping and stamping to the screeching music of a blind fiddler, who because of his handicap coupled with a viciously malicious expression seemed somehow to Miss Unwin a worse embodiment of evil than even the roaring drunk sailors and their women forming his audience.

On they went, hardly steadily since from time to time they were forced to a complete halt when some dancing circle lurched across their path.

A trio of seamen bore down on them with frightening directness, already beginning from a distance of ten yards or more to yell crude invitations. But by dint of swerving into the roadway they avoided the encounter.

A few yards further on, however, Miss Unwin had to drag Vilkins quickly into the mouth of a side street. A great lumbering drunk, a coal-whipper to judge by the glinting black dust clinging to his jacket and begrimed face and bare brawny forearms, was bearing down on them looking as if he was never going to take no for an answer. But the almost solid darkness of the lane, with its tottering buildings all but leaning into each other, seemed a worse danger. She came to a halt where some feeble light from the Highway still penetrated. The coal-whipper entered after them. Miss Unwin's fingertips sought the wooden handle of the kitchen-knife in her pocket.

But Vilkins just looked the huge fellow up and down.

'It's half a sov' to you, me lad,' she said. 'Not a penny less.'

'Half a sov'. For the likes o' you. Get out of it.'

The hulking coal-whipper turned and lurched away, guffawing like a maniac.

'I'll give 'im the likes o'you,' Vilkins exploded.

'No, come along. Come along. We're here for a purpose, don't forget.'

'Well, s'pose you're right. But I don't like being bested by a feller like that, I tell you.'

On they went.

Then a fight between two women blocked their path altogether with the happy, jeering crowd it had rapidly produced. 'Get yer nails in, Doll.' 'Kick 'er, Meg.' 'Give 'er a good 'un.' The set-to was drawing more onlookers by the minute, men, other women, children, laughing and shrieking.

'We'll 'ave to wait an' watch,' Vilkins whispered in her usual shower of spit. ''Less we do we'll attrac' attention.'

Miss Unwin realised that, once again, her companion and mentor in this underworld was right. She gritted her teeth and pretended to turn her full attention to the fighting women in the centre of the rough circle the onlookers had formed.

'What's it all about then?' Vilkins cheerfully demanded of a little wizened man in a sealskin cap standing beside her.

'Oh, they're always at it, them two,' he said. 'They both belongs to a sailor gone to Java for the spices. Leaves 'em 'ere, he does, both in the same bit of a house. But Meg, she don't want to spend what he leaves 'em with, an' Doll, she always starts to go through it like it was water. So the ship ain't 'ardly past Gravesend afore the two of 'em's at it tooth an' nail.'

'Which of 'em gets the best of it then?' Vilkins asked happily. 'Spend or save?'

The little man in the sealskin cap laughed.

'Sometimes one, sometimes the other,' he said. 'That's

123

what makes it so good. They're an even match. It's sometimes the one the peelers take in, when they comes at last, an' – Hey, look out.'

He had turned and was looking back up the road. Miss Unwin followed the direction of his gaze. Three policemen, bunched together for safety's sake, yet tall and looming in their black oilskin capes and tall hats, were slowly approaching. Round her, suddenly, she felt rather than saw the whole tight-knit crowd melt away. Meg – or was it Doll? – gave her opponent a last jabbing punch that laid her low and took to her heels with half a dozen raucously yelling urchins behind her.

'Come on,' said Vilkins.

Miss Unwin turned and they started off at a run. But in a moment better thoughts intervened and Miss Unwin took hold of Vilkins' arm and made her slow to a walk.

'I'd have more than a little explaining to do if we were taken up by the police here,' she said.

'Yer, you're right. Couple o' respectable girls we are, or nearly so, just going about our business.'

They went on at a more sedate pace, and almost at once caught sight of the hanging sign of the White Swan illuminated by a flaring gas-jet just beneath it. From the tall, board-fronted building the sound of singing and the music of a band could be heard.

'It shouldn't be far now,' Miss Unwin said, 'though I don't suppose we'll find a street sign.'

But in that she was unduly pessimistic. On an ancient piece of board at the second corner after they had passed the noise-rocked, brightly-lit Paddy's Goose there had been painted in crude letters, dripping from the brush, not 'Nile Street' but just the single word 'Nile'.

It was enough, however. They were within reach of their goal.

The little lane was as unlit as the turning had been where they had had their encounter with the coal-whipper. But this was a path Miss Unwin had got to take.

Far down it, Miss Unwin thought she detected a glimmer of light, perhaps from a feeble lantern.

'Look,' she said. 'There must be a house down there where someone's at home. Let's pray it's Mrs Meggs.'

'Well, if she's the skinflint you said she was,' Vilkins answered, 'I don't suppose she'll 'ave put light to so much as a candle.'

Miss Unwin refused to let herself be dismayed by this piece of lugubriousness.

'We shall see,' she said. 'Come on.'

They plunged into the black darkness of the lane. Beneath her feet Miss Unwin could feel the mud gripping and sucking. The smell was noisome, blotting out completely the tarry odours from the nearby shipping that had accompanied them up till now.

But, bit by bit as they felt their way along, the darkness yielded. Looking up, Miss Unwin could make out the dome of the sky above through the gap between the ramshackle buildings to either side, though this was hardly two yards wide. More than one pair of houses, indeed, was kept apart by beams of wood jammed across the lane.

A cat suddenly ran squawking from under their feet.

'Out arter rats, I shouldn't wonder,' Vilkins remarked cheerfully.

Miss Unwin felt less cheerful. But the tiny glimmer of light she had first seen was growing larger with each step they took. Now she could make out, peering ahead, that it came from a window down at ground level. It was so feeble, however, that she guessed it must come from a single tallow candle.

There were no other lights in the whole lane and Miss Unwin surmised that the people who lived in the hovels to either side found so little comfort indoors that they preferred to stay out as long as they could. No doubt many of them had been in that circle of jeering faces surrounding the two fighting women, the saver and the spender.

'Yes,' Vilkins said suddenly, 'looks as though it might be an ale house or something o' the sort.'

The light from the single window, though not much more than a yellowy glow, was, now that they were yet nearer, showing up something of the outside of the building. Miss Unwin, after a slithering pace or two more, was able to make out a board proclaiming 'Ales and Stout'.

Mrs Meggs's new home. The public house, such as it was, which it had been her ambition over the years to own. The house for which she had needed the small sum she had been left in old Mr Partington's Will. The house for which, perhaps, she had poisoned the old miser.

And now they were outside it.

There was a door of boards roughly knocked together, showing glints of light from the candle inside.

'Well, knock or something,' Vilkins said.

Chapter Thirteen

Miss Unwin had one secret question she intended to ask old Mr Partington's former housekeeper. She had worked it out from her reading of *Potherton on Poisons*. What had led her to it was asking herself how someone like Mrs Meggs could have obtained enough arsenic to kill the old miser. Going through the various sources of the poison which Professor Potherton had listed, she had been particularly struck by one. The professor, indeed, had drawn special attention to it as being the source most easily accessible 'to the generality'.

So easy was it to acquire, the professor had written, that he felt himself constrained to refer to it 'in the relative obscurity of Latin'. *Pedicae muscarum* was, he said, the nearest he could manage to describe it in the dead language.

And there he had ceased.

Miss Unwin had not yet in the course of self-education come to the gentlemen's preserve of Latin. Only the occasional phrase in general use was she conversant with. But she knew how to use a dictionary.

Five minutes' work gave her the answer. *Pedicae muscarum* or snares of flies. Otherwise, she realised, fly papers. By boiling a single *pedica muscarum*, Professor Potherton had written, a quantity of arsenic sufficient to effect death could be obtained.

So Miss Unwin came to the conclusion that if Mrs Meggs had indeed hastened the death of her employer in order to obtain the sum she needed to set her up in her long cherished public house, then by boiling fly papers she had most likely done it. Miss Unwin viewed Professor Potherton's careful use of the obscurity of the Latin language as so much shutting the stable door when horses galore had been stolen. She did not, of course, believe that Mrs Meggs, who could hardly read, had gone on the same hunt through the dictionary as herself. But she knew from her early days in the world down below how much knowledge exists there, more by far than is ever suspected by those sailing in the world above who believe nothing is known until it is in the pages of a book.

No, Mrs Meggs was perfectly likely to know that fly papers were a handy source of poison. And fly papers were easily to be bought. Fly-paper men, often with the sticky strips of glue-daubed paper wound round an old tall hat by way of advertising their wares, were a common sight.

So Miss Unwin saw the task that awaited her when she at last would find herself facing the cantankerous old crone who had ruled the kitchen of the Harrow Road house as being simple enough. She must insert into the conversation at some chosen moment a sharp question about fly papers. And then she must watch the old woman's face as intently as ever she watched the faces of her pupils to see whether they were comprehending what she was telling them. Armed then, perhaps, with the knowledge that the old woman was indeed guilty she could attack her as hard as she might.

Vilkins had asked her why she had not knocked at Mrs Meggs's door.

'No,' she replied, ending her time of doubt, 'I shall not knock. I shall go straight in.'

She put her hand to the rough boards in front of her and gave a sharp push.

The door yielded at once and they found themselves in the room that was soon to be the bar of Mrs Meggs's ale house. A trestle with planks of unplaned wood on it had been put up across one end and on that there burnt the single candle which had led them to the house. By its light old Mrs Meggs was peering ill-temperedly at a sheet of paper, apparently trying to make out what was written on it.

She looked up at the noise of their entrance. The candlelight caught the single white bristle of hair still protruding from her chin.

'Not open till –' she began.

Then, realising who her visitor was, she came to a dead halt.

'Good evening, Mrs Meggs,' Miss Unwin said. 'I hope I have not disturbed you. I have come to see that all is well with you. I am afraid you left Mr Partington's house in more of a hurry than he would have wished.'

The old woman glared at her.

'You're not wanted,' she said. 'Hussy. You poked your little nose in everywhere there. Don't come poking it in here.'

'But, Mrs Meggs, I hope I never interfered with your housekeeping at Harrow Road, and I have no intention of interfering here. I came only to see if you needed any help.'

'Then you can go back to where you came from. To his bed, I dare say. To his bed.'

Miss Unwin felt her anger rising. But she was determined not to be forced into a situation where she could not put her question about fly papers in a manner that would take the old housekeeper most by surprise.

She thought she saw a way towards her end.

'No,' she repeated, 'I came only to see if I could help. There is that paper there by the candle. Can I read it for you?'

'I can read what's to be read for myself.'

The old woman gave her a look of such malevolence that she almost quailed.

Out of the blue Vilkins came to her aid.

'Ain't no shame in not being able to make out other

129

people's letters,' she said, loudly and cheerfully. 'I can't hardly make out any meself, an' I'm 'appy as I am.'

'And who are you, barging in on an old woman?' Mrs Meggs retorted.

'This is Mary Vilkins,' Miss Unwin hastily explained. 'She has come to the house in your place.'

She was conscious that this was a departure from the truth. But to tell Mrs Meggs that the house she had ruled with such grim parsimony for so many years now boasted two servants might well rouse in her such a coil of malicious envy that any chance of putting the question about fly papers to good effect would be gone.

But Mrs Meggs was not to be so easily placated.

She gave the gaudily bonneted Vilkins a glare of anger.

'Then she ought to be back in her kitchen,' she said. ''Stead o' poking into my affairs. There's work enough to be done there, I can tell you.'

Was this another chance, Miss Unwin wondered.

'Why, yes,' she said. 'I always thought that you had more than enough to occupy you, what with waiting at table and cooking and cleaning all that big house.'

'And a sight more when you came,' the old woman snarled.

'I hope I did not make too much extra for you to do.'

'You did, didn't you? Wanting the parlour to give your lessons in and I don't know what else. Why those little brats had to be taught all the nonsense you put into their heads I don't know.'

'Well,' Miss Unwin answered, 'they are after all, you know, Mrs Meggs, the daughters of a gentleman. They must learn what it is proper for a lady to know.'

'Be wanting them to have a pianner next,' the old woman spat.

Miss Unwin had thought how in fact Richard Partington had already ordered a piano, and one of the finest and prettiest too. But, again, this was something best not told to the former housekeeper.

130

'Well,' she said, hoping to ease the talk into the direction she wanted, 'at least the girls no longer make work for you. I'm afraid they were dreadfully untidy.'

'Tidy, tidy. That's all you can think of. No harm in a bit of mess. Not when there's nothing but work and expense to clear it away.'

'Yes, but mess often leads to disease, you know. Dirt attracts flies, and –'

'And speakin' of mess,' the old woman brutally interrupted, 'you ain't been poking an' prying among the bits o' things I left, 'ave you? Them's not to be touched till I get back to take 'em, see.'

'I am sure that no one would disturb anything you were unable to take with you,' Miss Unwin answered, all the more coldly for her inner vexation that the subject of flies had just been pushed further off.

'Well, don't you go a-laying your thieving hands on 'em.'

'Oo are you calling a thief, I should like to know.'

Here was an insult to her friend altogether too much for honest Vilkins.

'I shall call a thief who I like. I dare say it's to see what more you can prig you came down here for.'

'That I have not,' Vilkins retorted, her dab of a nose taking on tones of the fieriest red. 'I come 'ere to –'

'Vilkins!'

The exclamation was all Miss Unwin could think of to halt her companion before she had blurted out the true reason for their visit.

'No,' Vilkins said, 'I ain't a-going to be called a thief by no old woman what's gone and –'

'No! Stop! Stop!'

Miss Unwin saw, with despair, that only one course was now left open to her. Retreat.

'Come, Vilkins,' she said, 'let us leave. That's the only way to deal with such accusations.'

For a moment she thought her friend was not going to

131

listen. But after a second or so of red-faced furious silence Vilkins did turn away.

'Yes,' she said, 'I won't stay 'ere to 'ear no talk like that. It's beneath me. That's what it is. Beneath me.'

And gaudy bonnet and all she swept to the door.

Miss Unwin stayed looking at Mrs Meggs. Had she missed altogether her chance of putting the old woman to the test? No, she must not let it go, however barely and baldly she now must ask her precious question.

'Then goodbye, Mrs Meggs,' she said. 'But, tell me one last thing. In what did you boil the fly papers?'

'Fly papers? Fly papers?' the old woman answered, peering at her from beneath her tangled eyebrows. 'I don't know what you mean about fly papers. I ain't never had no truck with fly papers. Cost more'n they're worth, they do.'

It was not the response Miss Unwin had hoped for. Far from it. But there was no more to be done.

She turned and left in Vilkins' wake.

Their journey out of the Ratcliff Highway was quicker than their journey into it and down dark malodorous Nile Street. But the ease with which they accomplished their departure was no pleasure to Miss Unwin. All she could think of was that the whole expedition with its very real dangers had been an entire waste of time. She had put a question to Mrs Meggs about fly papers, certainly. But it had had to be put so awkwardly, and it had elicited not the least glimmer of a guilty response.

Perhaps Mrs Meggs had obtained arsenic from some other source. It could be bought as rat poison after all. But an Act of Parliament of some thirty years before had laid down that it must then be mixed with a prescribed quantity of soot which ought to make it impossible to add in secret to human food.

So was Mrs Meggs innocent? Nasty and vicious though she was, it well might be that she had not sunk to murder. Perhaps she had been more content to wait to open her

132

public house than it had seemed. There were those extra large cups of tea she had continued to the last to bring to the old miser. She must have felt some deep regard for him.

But if she was not the person who had poisoned him, who was? It could not be Richard. It could not be. It must not be.

Then who could it be? The case against Captain Fulcher had certainly not been entirely disproved, for all that Inspector Redderman had treated it so lightly. Perhaps after all Jack Fulcher was the guilty one.

Or Cousin Cornelia? Could she have secretly introduced arsenic into the sherry her brother bought to take to the Harrow Road? It was surely possible. And she did have a reason for wishing that old Mr Partington was no longer living. If, as the little servant girl at the Captain's lodgings had indicated, she had foolishly given all her inheritance to her brother and had even had to let her house in the country and stay in the London she thought so dirty and unpleasant, then surely the prospect of marriage with Richard when he had inherited his father's wealth would be so much worth wishing for that she might well commit murder.

And murder would be needed. She could not have failed to have seen that the old miser would give his son nothing while he still had breath in his body. So had she, of her own accord and saying nothing to the brother she doted on, arranged that the breath should leave the old man's body?

Surely it was possible. And in any case there was no one else in the household or with regular access to it who could have committed the crime. No one else at all. So it had to be Miss Fulcher, if it was not the Captain or Mrs Meggs. But how could she prove any of this? How could she obtain even enough evidence to bring once again to Inspector Redderman?

She could think of no way.

As at last the two of them came out of the Ratcliff Highway into somewhat safer streets where a cab might be had, she heard faint in the distance behind her the sound of the shanty that was being sung by the circle of drunken seamen as they had arrived.

Oh, Mexico was covered in snow
The grub was bad and the pay was low

But Mexico is not covered in snow, she thought in a burst of fury with the whole place, and with herself. What was needed here was a sharp lesson in geography.

Chapter Fourteen

For most of the long cab journey from the East End through the City and Westminster and on through Bayswater till at last they came to the Harrow Road Vilkins sat as silent as Miss Unwin. Miss Unwin felt no inclination to berate her friend for the discomfiture they had experienced. With hindsight, she suspected that, whatever she had managed to say, old Mrs Meggs would not have yielded an inch. Her own silence was the result solely of feeling that she had now nowhere to look for evidence that would show Richard not to be guilty.

But, as at last their ancient growler turned into the Harrow Road, the reason for Vilkins' unusual lack of talk emerged.

'Unwin,' she suddenly burst out, 'I done it good an' proper, didn't I?'

'Do what, Vilkins dear?'

'Done it. Done it.'

Miss Unwin smiled in the straw-smelling darkness of the old cab.

'What "it" my dear? What "it" have you done?'

'Ruined it, spoilt it, upset the 'ole apple-cart of it.'

'Ah, our lack of success with Mrs Meggs. You're blaming yourself. But there's no need, really there isn't. I see now she was altogether too tough a bird to be caught in any springes we might set.'

'You sure?' said Vilkins, shedding doubt like a coster's donkey shedding its harness as soon as its cartload of vegetables was sold. 'Really sure? 'Course she was an old devil, like you'd said. What blooming cheek calling me a

135

thief, and you. I'd 'ave liked to 'ave given 'er a good clap round the chops, so I would.'

'Well, I doubt if that would have advanced matters very far. Think what would have happened if she had called the police.'

'Now, you must be off your rocker, Unwin. 'Er call in the peelers? She wouldn't never dare. An' they wouldn't never come. Not down Nile Street, they wouldn't.'

'Yes, I dare say you're quite right there. But all the same giving poor old Mrs Meggs a clap round the chops wouldn't have helped us.'

'It'd 'ave 'elped me. Given me some satisfaction.'

Vilkins fell back then into a silence that was happy.

But before their journey was quite done, while Miss Unwin was looking in her purse wondering whether the small supply of money that had been all she had dared take on so dangerous an errand would be enough to pay the cab-man, her companion broke out once more.

''Er an' 'er old bits o' things. I bet there isn't a rag worth 'aving among the lot o' them. An' telling me to keep my 'ands off of them.'

Miss Unwin looked up from her careful counting of coins.

'Not a rag worth having,' she echoed. 'I dare say you're right, my dear. Old Mrs Meggs wore the same garments, I swear, every day that I saw her in the house. But if she left behind nothing worth having, why was she so insistent that we were not to lay our hands on anything?'

'Spite, most likely,' Vilkins said.

'No. No, I think not.'

'Well, what was it then? If you're so clever.'

'Something . . . Something she did not want us to see.'

'What you mean?'

'Vilkins, what if there was something in old Mrs Meggs's room, something that she either forgot in the heat of her departure to take with her, or for some reason could not take?'

'What if there was?'

'Well, what if it was something – I don't know what – that when she saw us she realised might incriminate her?'

'What's incriminate?' said Vilkins.

'It's proof that someone is a criminal, Vilkins dear. Something that proves that. It could be proof that after all Mrs Meggs is a murderess.'

'Well then, we'll 'ave to look, won't we?' said Vilkins.

Look they did, before they had so much as taken off their bonnets. Miss Unwin paused only to make sure from a sleepy cook that the twins had stayed safely in their beds all the time she had been away.

'Mrs Miller,' she asked next, 'did you find anything belonging to Mrs Meggs when you moved into her room?'

'Move into her room?' the cook replied with some indignation. 'I tell you, Miss, I wouldn't no more have slept in that room than what I would fly.'

'Really? I knew nothing of this. What was wrong with the room?'

'Dirt,' said Mrs Miller. 'Dirt of ages and mess. Lord knows what she'd stored away in there, but it was too much for me to think of shifting. When we get that boy for the boots and knives that the Master said we could have, I'll get him to clear it all out for the rag-and-bone man. But till then, there it must stay. I'll not soil my hands with it.'

'No,' Miss Unwin said, 'but I will. This minute.'

And off she went with Vilkins, carrying one of the new bright brass oil-lamps that Richard Partington had bought by the dozen, to inspect the old housekeeper's lair.

It was a strange sight that met their eyes. Little wonder, Miss Unwin thought, that Mrs Miller had refused so much as to go in.

Up each wall from floor to ceiling there were stacked and piled discarded household objects of every sort. Even the one small window near the top of the back wall was three-quarters obscured, and further layers were piled in front of those already up against the walls.

'Why,' Vilkins said in tones of deep awe, 'she must of kep' every blessed bottle that come into the 'ouse the 'ole time she was 'ere.'

'I do believe you're right, my dear. She seems to have had an especial fondness for bottles. I wonder at it. She could have had many a halfpenny selling them at the door.'

'P'raps she was a-saving 'em up, to add to 'er nest-egg,' Vilkins suggested.

'You may be right. And perhaps, after all, that's why she wanted us not to interfere with them. That and no more.'

Her heart began to sink.

'Well, I don't know,' Vilkins said. 'If you ask me you was right in the first place. She went on so about the blessed things. Somewhere among 'em, like as not, there's something what you called incrimerating.'

Miss Unwin looked at the dusty array, the jars and bottles, the gallipots and pipkins, the flagons and carboys.

'But, oh, Vilkins,' she said, 'where are we going to begin? How can we find the one thing in all this mess that Mrs Meggs wanted to keep from us, if it's there at all?'

Vilkins scratched her head under her garish bonnet.

'Begin at the beginning, I s'pose,' she said.

'No,' Miss Unwin answered, suddenly seized with a notion. 'No, it should be begin at the end.'

'Begin at the end? That's daft, Unwin.'

'Oh, no, it isn't, my dear. Don't you see? Whatever it is that Mrs Meggs doesn't want anybody to know about, always supposing there is something, whatever it is is likely to be something that she used recently. The bottle or jar or whatever it turns out to be which she used somehow to give old Mr Partington the arsenic.'

'All right then. But 'ow do we tell where the end is what we got to begin at?'

'Simple, I think. We look for the least dusty objects we can see.'

'All right.'

Vilkins stooped and held the lamp low down near the floor. At once it was obvious that some of the bottles and jars lined up in the outer row were less dust-covered than others.

'Yes,' she said, 'look at these. Cleaning stuff, though you wouldn't of thought any o' that had been used 'ere for many a long day. But 'ere it is, that old Cor Rosy Subjec' mate.'

'Oh, Vilkins,' Miss Unwin began, 'you should say –'

And then she stopped.

Her eye had been caught by a comparatively clean and sparkling bottle standing next to the cleaning fluid ones which Vilkins had been commenting on. And the name on its label, written in the flourishing, confident handwriting of a chemist's shop proprietor, was ringing loud and furious bells in her head.

Fowler's Solution. As directed.

Surely she had come across that name somewhere quite recently, and in a context that was somehow relevant to her present purpose.

'But where?

'Vilkins,' she asked, 'have you ever heard of Fowler's Solution?'

'Something to do with catching fowl, I should think.'

Miss Unwin laughed.

And as she did so the place where she had seen those words in their correct meaning came floating back into her mind. In *Potherton on Poisons*, no less. Fowler's Solution was one of the many sources of arsenic that the learned professor had listed. It had come far down in his tables since it did not contain more than one per cent of arsenic trioxide in a neutral base. But it was there. Fowler's Solution was a standard remedy for a certain mouth

139

infection and it was also – Miss Unwin began to feel excitement pulsing through her – a general tonic. Had Mrs Meggs, always concerned about her Master's health, first just taken to adding Fowler's Solution to his tea each evening? Was that why she had invariably given him that extra large cup?

Hastily Miss Unwin ran her eye over more of the serried ranks of bottles and jars. And, sure enough, the bottle of Fowler's Solution with its boldly written chemist's label was only one of a dozen or more of the same sort.

So Mrs Meggs had had arsenic at her disposal, and if she had after all made up her mind to the evil act could she not have given old Mr Partington a much stronger dose or doses than the great Fowler had prescribed when he had invented the solution that bore his name?

Inspector Redderman could hear from the rabbit-skin man that Mrs Meggs had reason to want her employer to die, once he had been told that there existed a source of poison under the old crone's control. Surely then he would see her at the very least as his prime suspect?

And he would release Richard.

Miss Unwin wondered what time of night it was. Would it be too late to go to the Inspector now? At this moment?

She hurried back to the kitchen where an old, loud-ticking clock stood on the mantel above the range.

Mrs Miller had gone to bed and had left no light in the big room. But there was a glow reflected from the dying fire. Miss Unwin reached up, took down the clock and peered hard.

Tick. Tock. Tick. Tock. At last her eyes grew accustomed enough to the gloom to make out the two big black hands.

Midnight.

Midnight already. Where had the time gone to? And, of course, at midnight Inspector Redderman would be safe in his bed. And Richard, poor Richard, would be lying on the hard bench in his cell, all unknowing that he need lie there no longer.

If Inspector Redderman took the sensible view.

But that would have to be tomorrow.

'Vilkins,' Miss Unwin called to her friend still in Mrs Meggs's bottle-ranged lair. 'Dear, we should go to bed now, I must be up betimes in the morning.'

'Lord, yes. I'm sleepy as a squirrel.'

But if Vilkins was sleepy, and doubtless slept, Miss Unwin was by no means so. She may have dozed unwittingly for an hour or two. But next morning as soon as it was light she got out of bed convinced that she had not closed her eyes once all night.

Over and over in her mind she had rehearsed what she was going to say to Inspector Redderman. She had convinced herself before she had been in bed a quarter of an hour that all would depend on the way she was able to put her case. That she seemed to have strong facts to offer the Inspector, facts that ought to speak for themselves, she soon forgot. No, it was the way she would marshal her evidence, the logic she herself would present, that was going to mean freedom for Richard or trial for his life. She felt utterly convinced of it.

And, worse, before she lapsed unknowingly into the first of her short spells of sleep, she had convinced herself, too, that if Richard were brought to trial he would be found guilty. The fact of his complete innocence would not be enough. Inspector Redderman would amass such a pile of evidence against him, would brief the prosecuting counsel with such cleverness, that Richard would stand no chance. A great injustice would be done, and the man she loved would perish on the gallows, condemned as the murderer of his own father.

So it was in no very fit state that she set out next day to go to the police office.

Her head ached. Her mouth felt dry. The tea that she

141

had swallowed at breakfast had seemed brackish as sea-water. Her limbs were heavy. And as for her thoughts, they might, she believed, be so many whirling sheets of paper tossed in a gale so far were they from being in any order.

Not that she had not tried to marshal them. She had risen much too early to go round to the police office, and so, once again neglecting the poor twins, she had on the excuse of having the headache taken half an hour in privacy to attempt to get her case as well put together as she could. She had sat and written out the heads of what she had to say, and then had solemnly gone over them one by one fleshing them out with words. At the time it had seemed to her that she had got the whole into very tolerable order. But now, walking leadenly along the Harrow Road in the direction of the police station, she found she was unable to remember a single one of all the forceful, logical sentences she had put together.

She halted and searched in her pocket for the little memorandum sheet she had made up. She took it out and read it over. Yes, that was what she had to say.

Standing just where she was, she screwed the paper into a roll and pushed it into her glove and in her mind began her recitation to Inspector Redderman once again. 'Inspector, I have come across, largely by accident, some important information which I think you should have. I know that once before I came to you –' No. No, that particular plea she had resolved to keep to the end, if it was still needed. So what was going to come after . . . *information which I think you should have?*

Her mind was blank and she felt her head jangling as if some harsh irregular music was going on inside it. She opened her fist to consult her cues again. The wretched sheet of paper was so crushed as to be unreadable.

'Thank you, lady, thank you. A poor man's blessing on you. First of the day and good luck it'll bring you.'

What was this?

A strident voice in her ear.

She looked round. There was an organ-grinder at the pavement's edge, his circular drum of an instrument perched on its single stick and on his shoulder, trembling with either perpetual excitement or an ague, his monkey.

That had been the music she had believed was solely in her head. And the man must have thought she had stopped for him and had a coin in her glove instead of that terrible screwed-up paper.

Hastily she opened her purse, found a halfpenny, put it in the fellow's little cloth bag and walked off. Then, before she rightly knew it, she found herself on the steps of the police office.

No help for it now. She could not turn tail. However much of a jumble her once carefully arranged thoughts were, she could not decline to put them in front of Inspector Redderman and leave Richard still at his mercy.

'Yes, mum,' the sergeant at the counter said. 'Inspector Redderman's been here this quarter of an hour. Punctual to the dot is the Inspector, never known him miss.'

'Then I can see him?'

'I'll have you shown up straight away, mum. You've been to see the Inspector before, ain't you? About the vicious murder at the pin works, if I mistake not.'

'Then please have me taken to him,' Miss Unwin said in a cold fury.

So, without a chance to pause and try for a last time to get some order into her thoughts, she found herself once again facing Inspector Redderman.

He was alone in his room, a quiet figure seated at that bare table on which everything was arranged with such exact neatness. It was neatness and exactitude reflected very well in the man himself with his tightly buttoned coat, his neckcloth neatly arranged to the last fold, his unemphatic features and the short grey crop of his hair.

'Miss Unwin,' he said as soon as she was shown in. 'You have something new to tell me?'

There was an edge of doubt in his tone. Miss Unwin decided that he thought that a person like herself, a woman, could well be so foolish as to come to him a second time with no more to say than she had had at the first.

And with that suspicion all the wild jumble of thoughts that had lain in her head ordered themselves as if at a touch of a master conjuror's wand.

'Yes, Mr Redderman,' she said, 'I have come across, largely by accident, some important new information which I think you should have.'

After that there rolled out, as neat and precise as the Inspector himself could have made them, the various points that she had intended he should learn from her.

He listened gravely and without showing any sign of either liking or disliking what he was hearing. At last she finished.

'Poisons,' he said. 'You appear to know a great deal more about such matters than young ladies should.'

It was not the response Miss Unwin had expected. But at least, she thought, he seems to have accepted that the argument I have put has some validity.

'My knowledge is easily enough explained,' she replied. 'I have made it my business in the past few days to acquaint myself with what I could of the subject.'

'Indeed? And how have you done that, Miss?'

'By reading *Potherton on Poisons*,' Miss Unwin replied, with not a little pride.

'*Potheterton on Poisons*, eh?'

The Inspector seemed impressed.

'A great work,' he went on. 'Indeed, Professor Potherton is the authority on the subject.'

He cast her a quick shrewd glance.

'But how did you come to lay your hands on such a volume?' he asked.

144

'I – I purchased it, Inspector. From a bookshop in Oxford Street.'

'Indeed? And paid a pretty price for it, no doubt. Now, I wonder why you should have done that. Not many governesses of my acquaintance would be so willing to sacrifice three guineas or more of their hard-earned stipend.'

'I – I felt an obligation to do so. To – To do what I could to relieve – to relieve my employer of a shadow unjustly cast upon him.'

'Very commendable. A young lady to go to such lengths for a gentleman who has had her in his employ, if I'm right, only some four or five months.'

Miss Unwin felt she had no answer to that. And she was sure, too, that Inspector Redderman had drawn his own conclusions as to her motive. Nor was it a false deduction.

'So, Miss Unwin,' he went on, having looked at her so hard and long that she had not been able to prevent her gaze dropping. 'So let us come to the bottles of Fowler's Solution. Found in the room formerly occupied by Mrs Meggs, you say?'

'I do. To my mind they are strong evidence.'

'Oh, yes. No doubt to your mind they are.'

Miss Unwin bristled.

'Are you telling me, Inspector, that such evidence means nothing?'

'No. No, not at all. Such evidence would mean a very great deal, if you had not thought that it would do so in advance.'

For a moment Miss Unwin did not understand what had been said. Then she saw it.

She almost leapt up from her chair.

'Are you saying that I am a liar? Do you mean to imply that I have planted evidence against an innocent old woman?'

The Inspector was not one whit discomposed.

'It is something which a man of my experience might expect,' he replied, 'when he has cause to believe that the person putting that evidence in front of him is deeply interested in the gentleman hitherto held for inquiry.'

'But I – But I –'

Miss Unwin fell silent. She was not going to deny the truth of what the Inspector had said. That would be to deny the love she felt for Richard Partington. But almost equally she felt that she could not admit that love. To do so would be to admit to the Inspector that his evil suspicions might be justified.

Almost she got up and left the room without a word. But her common sense asserted itself just in time. She thought what the situation really was and, after a moment's pause, she told Inspector Redderman.

'You are quite mistaken, sir, if you think that I have done anything as criminal as to falsify evidence. I would scorn to do so. But, more, I think I can show you conclusively that nothing of the kind has taken place.'

'Indeed?'

'Yes, indeed, Mr Inspector. It so happens that the new cook at the house, a person who could have no possible interest in telling other than the truth, looked into that room of Mrs Meggs's on her arrival. She saw it was so cluttered with bottles and jars that she refused to use it. But she can tell you that nothing has been disturbed in there. You can go yourself and see the evidence, a number of bottles labelled Fowler's Solution. Then I hope you will be convinced.'

Inspector Redderman did not immediately answer. He sat, still as ever, and simply gave the matter thought.

Then at last he spoke.

'Very well, Miss Unwin,' he said. 'I shall have to verify what you have told me, of course. But I can see no reason why Mr Richard Partington should remain at the police office any longer.'

Chapter Fifteen

Richard looked tired and not a little ill when he was
brought up from some nether region of the police station
to be reunited with Miss Unwin. Seeing him pale and
drawn, she wanted to take him by his hands and tell him
that all would be well from now on. She wanted, indeed,
in some deeper part of her mind to do more, to take him in
her arms.

But in the lobby of the police station with Inspector
Redderman, grey and self-contained, looking on she
could do neither of those things.

'Good morning, sir,' she said. 'I trust you are none the
worse for your long stay here.'

'Miss Unwin,' he said, surprised that she should be
there. 'This – This is an unexpected pleasure.'

The Inspector stepped half a pace forward.

'Not really unexpected, Mr Partington,' he said. 'I
think I can say that you owe your being at liberty to step
outside now almost entirely to this young lady. She has
been unremitting in her efforts to persuade me that I
should look elsewhere in this business. Altogether
unremitting.'

And Miss Unwin saw him regard Richard with a look so
keen that the least betrayal of feelings would not escape
him.

But it was no minute sign that Richard gave of what his
feelings were. He coloured up in an instant. A look of
warm gratitude shone from his eyes.

'Miss Unwin,' he said. 'Harriet, how can I ever thank
you?'

Inspector Redderman permitted himself a small inclination of the head as much as to say *Ah, yes, so I was right*.

'I should not, if I were you, express too fervant thanks,' he said drily. 'I feel bound to warn you that, though I see the need at present to conduct investigations elsewhere, I do not necessarily consider I have asked you everything I may wish to.'

With that quietly spoken warning singing in their ears, Richard and Miss Unwin left the police station.

Miss Unwin turned in the direction of the house and the pin works expecting that they would walk along there together. But Richard, with a sudden burst of energy, vigorously hailed a passing hansom.

'Surely, sir,' Miss Unwin said, 'it is a distance that can easily be walked? Or do you feel truly ill?'

She looked at him with quick anxiety. But there was no sign on his face that he was more than merely tired, and indeed already he had regained much of his colour.

'Ah, but no, my dear,' he said in answer. 'We are not going tamely back to the house. Far from it. This is no moment for quiet regularity. Can you guess where I intend to take you?'

Miss Unwin could not. No idea came into her head of where Richard, so soon after his release from that long series of questionings, could possibly want to go. Once, yes, before his father's death when the house had been so cold and uncomfortable, he might have wanted to visit a Turkish bath. But now there was no reason why he should not bath to his heart's content in water as hot as he liked in his own home, and drink tea there and eat a good breakfast beside a fire if he wanted one.

'You cannot guess?' Richard asked with a smile.

'No, sir, not possibly.'

'Not after what Inspector Redderman has just told me about you?'

'No, sir.'

148

'Why, you goose, I am going to take you to buy you a present. The best there is to be had. We'll go to Asprey's.'

'To Asprey's, the jeweller's?'

Miss Unwin felt altogether dazed by this impetuosity. She hardly knew what to think. That Richard should be so eager to show his regard for her – no, she corrected herself, surely his love for her – made her glow and glow with pleasure. But, without at first quite knowing why, she did not altogether like the manner in which he was proposing to show this gratitude, this love.

Words alone, she thought, as gradually she came to terms with the whirling feelings inside her, words of thanks alone would have been enough. More than enough. To hear Richard voice his thanks for what little she had done for him with all the warmth she recognised that he was showing in this other madder enterprise: that would have satisfied her every dream. But to hear him proposing to spend some large sum on a piece of jewellery from the shop which she understood to be the best and most expensive in all London: it was something she could not find wholly pleasing.

But the hansom had come to a halt beside them in the roadway. Richard had opened its doors. He put out his arm to hand her up the iron step. How could she disappoint him?

Meekly she allowed herself to be installed in the fly-away vehicle. A moment later Richard was there beside her. A moment more and he was tapping on the roof above them in signal to the cabbie behind to start. And then they were bowling along with all the exhilaration that a ride in a hansom can possess when there is little traffic to impede its way.

Then they were in Bond Street and the vehicle had halted outside the tall impressive building that housed the jewellers, and its wide plate-glass windows with their discreet displays of fabulous gems were glittering in the May sunshine before her.

'Rich – Mr Partington,' she managed to say before she had stepped down from the lightly swaying cab. 'Mr Partington, please do not think I am not grateful for the offer you are making me. But – But, truly, I do not want anything. I do not feel it is right that you should give me anything.'

Except, except, she added secretly to herself, except your love.

'Nonsense, nonsense,' Richard answered.

And he held out his hand with such firm gaiety that she could not do other than put hers into it and allow him to help her down on to the pavement.

'Please, sir,' she said, 'it is not nonsense. Very well, if you will, I acknowledge that I may have done something to secure your release from Inspector Redderman's interrogation. But whatever I have done, I have done willingly and would do again without a second thought.'

'But you have done for me what no one else would do. You have done what no one else could have done, I am certain. And I will reward you. Indeed, whatever bauble I find for you here will not be half enough to show my – my feelings.'

It was these last two words that were Miss Unwin's undoing. That Richard should wish to show her not simply gratitude, but feelings. She felt no longer able to resist anything. For what else could he have meant by the word than feelings of love?

Before she knew it she was in the shop, and before they had been inside its doors five minutes the top of the glass showcase in front of her was strewn with a profusion of jewelled objects glinting richly against a thrown-down velvet cloth.

'Now, choose,' Richard said. 'And do not hesitate. Whatever catches your fancy you shall have. Take two, if you want. Do take any two that you cannot choose between.'

'But, Mr Partington –'

'No. No buts. Or only: But I would like three. That is the furthest I am prepared to allow you.'

Miss Unwin desperately wanted to say that if she were being given a true choice, then she wanted nothing. But the shopman was standing there, leaning a little forward with obsequious interest, and she felt she could not engage in a battle of contradiction.

She looked down again at the glittering display. Was there something, one thing, that seemed less costly than the others? Was there not something that looked decently modest?

Her eye fell on a little heart-shaped olivine brooch surrounded by a tiny border of pearls. It was very pretty. If she had been a rich woman she could have seen herself wanting such an object. And besides it was heart-shaped. And it really seemed to be the least valuable object in front of her.

She wished violently that the shopman had murmured prices as one by one at Richard's instigation he had brought out the wealth the place possessed. But he had been discretion itself.

'Now, choose. One, two or three. Choose.'

'Well, if you insist. Then – Then this.'

She picked up the brooch. It really was delightfully pretty.

'But you have chosen the very smallest item,' Richard said. 'Add something else to it. This necklace, now would not that suit you admirably?'

'No, sir, it would not.'

'Not? But why ever do you say so? It seems to me that it would set off your features to a nicety.'

'As to that, sir, I cannot be the judge. But it would not suit me because it is a necklace of diamonds.'

'And they would gain lustre from your wearing them.'

Richard's eyes shone in his round, snub-nosed face, and Miss Unwin felt for him at that moment such a gush of love that tears came.

But she was not going to yield.

'No, Mr Partington,' she said. 'Because you have made such a point of it I will accept this brooch. But nothing more. Nothing. Do not press me, or I shall refuse even this charming thing.'

'Very well, you obdurate person,' Richard said.

He turned to the shopman, pulling out his newly acquired chequebook with a flourish.

'How much do I owe you?' he asked.

'Just fifty guineas, sir.'

'Fifty –'

Miss Unwin had to rein herself sharply back. But she longed to heap reproaches on the giver of the gift. Fifty guineas. It was a sum out of all proportion to anything she had done to earn it.

But Richard, without a qualm, was writing out the cheque.

Miss Unwin sat in silence in the hansom that whisked them back to the Harrow Road. She hoped that Richard, who had been so absurdly, so ridiculously, generous was taking her silence for a gratitude that had deprived her of words. But the truth was that speech had been taken from her by the turmoil of mixed feelings she was experiencing.

At the house Richard asked her to stay with him while he ate a late breakfast. But Miss Unwin was adamant.

'I am here as governess to your daughters, Mr Partington,' she said. 'And I am afraid that of late I have been scandalously neglectful of my duty towards them.'

So she spent the rest of the day no longer as an investigator of crime but as a simple governess. And very glad she was to be able to do that. For one thing she found the many hours that Louisa and Maria had been made to sit alone studying the tasks she had given them had had as bad an effect as she had feared. In the months she had been in the house she had, she prided herself, gradually brought them both from a state of semi-savagery to taking a real interest in what she had to teach. But it had been hard work, and their attention to their lessons had always been precarious. Now they had lapsed.

Miss Unwin had been aware of their falling into bad ways even before she had been temporarily not a governess but an investigator. There had been signs of a slackness she deplored, but she had put it out of her mind when Richard himself was in jeopardy. There had been worse signs, too, of a new greediness despite the gifts their father had showered them with before his incarceration. The more they had received the more Louisa at least had seemed to want. But, again, Miss Unwin had shut her eyes.

'Louisa, pay attention,' she said now, for the fifth or sixth time that morning. 'If you will not listen, you cannot learn.'

'But, Miss Unwin, Papa is back today. We really ought to have a holiday.'

'What nonsense. Just because your father has been away on business and has now returned there is no need for you to break off the course of your studies.'

'But it has been broken off, Miss Unwin,' Maria pointed out more quietly. 'You have scarcely been with us to give us any lessons for a week.'

'Well, no, Maria, it has not been as long as that. But I agree I have been absent more than I would have liked. However, it was necessary and there it is.'

Then she saw Louisa give her twin a glance which clearly boded some naughtiness.

'Now, Louisa. *La plume de ma tante est sur la table*. Translate, please.'

'But, Miss Unwin, *le père de nous est* – or rather he has been – *dans prison*.'

'You were not meant to know that,' Miss Unwin burst out before she could stop herself. 'How did you know it? And, besides, it isn't true.'

'Oh, Miss Unwin, we never thought you would tell a fib,' Louisa said with great cheerfulness.

'I am not – No, dear, what I have said is nothing but the plain truth. Your father has not been in prison. True, he has been kept at the police office. Your grandfather died in a mysterious manner, and of course the police have to inquire into it all. But it has been no more than that.'

'But he was locked up,' Maria observed.

'Well, yes, I suppose that he was prevented from returning home. But that was all a dreadful mistake. The Inspector, Inspector Redderman, has now come clearly to the conclusion that, of course, your father could have had nothing to do with the dreadful thing that has happened.'

Miss Unwin, even as she spoke, knew that what she was saying was not the exact truth. Inspector Redderman had made a point of indicating that he still considered it possible that Richard had been responsible for the crime. But that was simply not the case. It could not be true. So there was no harm, surely, in softening a little the Inspector's warning.

'Well, in any case,' Louisa said, 'if Papa was locked up and has now been let out we ought to have a holiday.'

'But you will not. You have already missed too many lessons, and we are going to make up for lost time as hard as we can.'

'Well, you may be going to as hard as you can, Miss,' the irrepressible Louisa said. 'But as for us, well, we'll just have to wait and see.'

But at least she bent her head over her French book once again.

So the rest of the day passed quietly enough. They all dined together, and Richard cut such prodigious slices of mutton that Miss Unwin wondered whether her plate would hold them all. And afterwards she made an excuse of lessons to prepare for the next day and re-treated to her room. There, with wonderful relief, she set aside *Potherton on Poisons* and took up instead her French grammar. She was not so far ahead of her pupils in knowledge of that language that she

154

could afford to forget her own studies.

The next day seemed to pass as easily and well as the day before it. Life was back to its ordinary way, Miss Unwin felt. True, old Mr Partington's death was as much of a mystery as ever. But she presumed Inspector Redderman was making inquiries in Nile Street. Perhaps he had already arrested Mrs Meggs and they would only be told of it when it pleased him to do so. Certainly the day before, as she had learnt from Vilkins, he had paid a prompt visit to the kitchen quarters and had carried out a long examination of Mrs Meggs's old room before sealing it under lock and key.

So perhaps it was all over.

Then quite late in the afternoon, after she had brought the girls back from their walk and was reading to them, Vilkins knocked at the door.

'Yes, Mary, what is it?'

'Please, Miss,' Vilkins said in her best parlour-maid manner, which was not very much of a parlour-maid manner but sufficed. 'Please, Miss, you're wanted by the Master. Down in the drawing room – and he's in a taking about something.'

'That will do, Mary.'

But by delivering this mild rebuke Miss Unwin failed to learn that Richard was not alone in the drawing room. She entered only slightly puzzled as to what he could urgently want at an hour when he knew the girls' lessons were not quite over. And there standing gravely by the fireplace was Inspector Redderman with beside him, more grave and much more rotund, Doctor Sumsion.

'Miss Unwin,' Inspector Redderman said without preliminary, 'Mr Partington thinks that you should be present to hear certain matters which have come to light.'

'Yes, Inspector?'

'Perhaps you would be as well to be seated.'

'Very well, if what you have to say will take some time.'

Miss Unwin chose the first chair to hand and sat.

'Doctor,' the Inspector went on, having seemed to take charge, 'you had better say what has to be said.'

'If you wish it.'

Doctor Sumsion gave a little cough.

'I understand, Miss Unwin,' he began, 'that it was you who pointed out to the Inspector here the presence in this house of a considerable number of empty bottles that had once contained Fowler's Solution.'

'I did, sir.'

'Yes, well, I am sure it was most perspicacious of you.'

The doctor paused and looked at the rich new Turkey carpet at his feet.

'But is that all you have to say, sir?'

'No. No, it is not. Ahem. The fact is that I have to make something of a confession.'

'Indeed, Doctor? But I am sure it cannot be to any very grave crime.'

The doctor flushed angrily.

'It is not to any crime whatsoever,' he said. 'It is to – to a certain lack of foresight, if you will. Hardly more than that.'

Again he paused. But this time Miss Unwin thought better of urging him on. At last with another little cough he resumed.

'The fact of the matter is that, although I undertook myself since it is somewhat of an interest of mine to carry out the tests on the – er – cadaver to ascertain whether death was due to arsenic, I – I . . .'

'That is Marsh's Test?' Miss Unwin inquired.

Doctor Sumsion looked very put out.

'How – How does a young lady like you know of such things?' he demanded.

'I have made it my business to learn, sir,' Miss Unwin replied. 'I obtained Professor Potherton's book on poisons and read as much of it as I was able.'

The doctor looked at her down his nose.

'I would not have expected a lady would have been able

to read such a work at all,' he said. 'However, that is scarcely the point.'

'The point being,' Inspector Redderman put in, 'that Doctor Sumsion unfortunately did not draw all the conclusions he might have from his tests. Since you suggested the possible source of the poison to us, Miss Unwin, we have thought it advisable to consult Professor Potherton himself.'

'And, well, the fact of the matter is,' the doctor resumed, 'that the amount of arsenic – er – present was not enough to have brought about death. It was, however, consonant with a small regular ingestion of arsenic in the form of Fowler's Solution, which, as perhaps you may not know, is prescribed as a tonic.'

Miss Unwin did, of course, know about Fowler's Solution as a tonic. But something else a great deal more pressing than any chagrin she might have felt at the doctor's repeated assumption of her ignorance was now in the forefront of her mind.

She turned to the Inspector.

'Mr Redderman,' she said, 'does this mean that some other poison was responsible for Mr Partington's death and that such ideas as we may have had about it are no longer valid?'

'Yes,' said the Inspector. 'That is precisely what it does mean, Miss Unwin. Some poison other than arsenic was employed.'

Chapter Sixteen

Miss Unwin felt her whole world turned topsy-turvy by what she had heard. She longed to be able to go somewhere quiet and work out in peace all the logical implications. But she had to stay a good while longer in the drawing room and listen to Doctor Sumsion telling and re-telling the details of it all in an effort to put his amateur scientific efforts into a better light. Inspector Redderman said almost nothing while the doctor was doing his best to alter the facts, and Richard was totally silent.

His air of utter crestfallenness, indeed, added another strand, and a strong one, to the tangled web which Miss Unwin wanted so badly to have time and peace to unravel.

It was only when Doctor Sumsion had at last put things as much to his satisfaction as he could with the declaration that 'of course even Professor Potherton has not yet concluded all the tests necessary to ascertain just what the deleterious element is' that he eventually ceased to speak.

Then the Inspector put in his word.

'So I will bid you goodbye, Mr Partington,' he said. 'But I would be failing in my duty if I let you believe that I do not expect to see you again. We are back to where we were before, you know. And to me the answer that provides fewest difficulties must always seem the likeliest.'

Richard drew himself up to his full, not very great, height.

'I think, Inspector,' he said, 'that I have told you everything you have any right to demand of me.'

'That may be so, sir. But I will not baulk the issue. This is a matter where I, and not you, decide what rights I have.'

And with that he picked up his hat, turned on his heel and marched off. Doctor Sumsion, having looked once round the room and perceived he was the sole visitor, uttered a word of farewell and departed in his turn.

'Oh, Miss Unwin,' Richard said dolefully, the moment the door had closed behind him. 'What shall we do now? We are just where we were. The man is right. All your efforts on my behalf seem to have come to nothing.'

'Then perhaps you should take back the present you pressed on me for those efforts,' Miss Unwin said, uttering in her confusion of mind the first words that came into her head. 'I dare say Messrs Asprey will return the money you paid for it.'

At least, she thought to herself, one piece of good may come out of this.

'No. No, never,' Richard answered. 'Miss Unwin, Harriet, what you did you did. That, later, things came to this pass takes away none of the merit of your actions.'

Miss Unwin looked at him. His open round face was suffused with new colour. He was plainly in the grip of high emotion.

In two seconds more, she thought to herself, he will make me a formal proposal.

'Sir, sir,' she broke out. 'I must – the children. I must return to them. I left them without any task to do. They will be up to mischief. I must go.'

She hurried to the door, wrenched it open and ran upstairs.

All she knew at this moment was that, for whatever reason, she did not want to hear what Richard Partington was plainly on the point of saying to her. It had been her hope, hardly admissible even to herself in her most private thoughts, that Richard might utter to her the words he had been on the point of saying just a moment before. They would have answered her deepest hopes. But she knew, too, with iron certainty that for some reason or none she did not want to hear them now.

And, besides, the children really might be up to some mischief. They had, after all, been left abruptly and without having been given anything to do. Thanks, too, to Doctor Sumsion's exculpatory burblings, she herself had been away much longer than she had thought likely.

So duty did call.

It was not much mischief that she found the twins in, merely that they were eating sugar-plums from an enormous box which their father had bought in Bond Street after getting his much more expensive gift for their governess. But it was within an hour of dinner, and the girls knew well that at such a time sweet things were forbidden.

'I hoped you could be trusted, even though I had set you no task,' Miss Unwin said, as she took the box of plums and locked it away.

'But you did set us no task,' Louisa answered, 'so really it is you who should be having your sugar-plums locked away.'

'No, Louisa.'

Louisa did not continue. She could recognise the note of danger. But Maria, always the quieter follower yet with a strain of loyalty in her that was willing to venture into risk, did not let the argument drop.

'But, Miss, it isn't fair that we should be punished when we had not been helped to be good.'

'Is it not, Maria? Ask yourself that again.'

Solemnly and in silence Maria did ask herself the question. And came to the same conclusion.

'I still think it's unfair, Miss. You know we had a very hard life till – till Grandpapa died. We did. You know we did. So we ought to have more help than other little girls.'

'Yes,' added Louisa, coming back into the fray refreshed, 'especially from a governess papa took on particularly to help us. And especially when he gives her gifts.'

Miss Unwin felt outraged.

That gift, that so pretty brooch with its heart shape outlined in tiny pearls, she had hidden away at once in the back of the drawer in her room where she kept her handkerchiefs and collars. Neither of the girls had any business to go prying there. And yet they had done so, and had guessed how she had come by such a valuable object.

What more had they guessed? Had they jumped to the real reason why their father had made her the gift? Not because she had done something to free him from Inspector Redderman's clutches but because he was going to ask her to become their stepmother.

'Louisa,' she said, trying to restrain the anger that boiled up in her. 'I had made up my mind to restore the sugar-plums to you. Maria's reasoning seemed to me very good. But after what I have just learnt you will not see that box again for one whole week. And you may think yourselves lightly dealt with if that is all the punishment you receive.'

Silence then. A silence between the three of them that lasted until each of the girls was in bed with the curtains drawn round her.

It was only then that Miss Unwin thought she could have her longed-for opportunity of thinking hard and carefully about the consequences of the unexpected reversal of all her hopes that prosy old Doctor Sumsion had brought about. Once again she made the excuse to Richard of needing to prepare the twins' lessons for next day. She saw he was pathetically anxious for her company after dinner, but she steeled her heart.

Until she had had that long session of hard thought, until she had settled the pros and cons thoroughly in her own mind, she dare not risk what a stay in Richard's company might bring.

It might bring – if she spoke truly to herself she was

162

certain that it would bring – those words that Richard had been about to pronounce immediately after Doctor Sumsion's visit. And though she longed to hear those words and knew her answer would surely be a fervent 'Yes', she knew, too, that she was not yet ready to hear them. She would not be ready until she had straightened out two things in her head. First, what should she think and do about the new situation that had arisen over old Mr Partington's death. And, second, that awkward burr of doubt which had appeared in her mind almost at the moment of her triumph in securing Richard's release, the unease she felt over the absurdly expensive gift he had thrust upon her.

But she was not to get her period of quiet reflection.

''Ere, is what I 'eard true?'

Vilkins had thrust open the door of her room.

'Vilkins. How – how do you know there is anything to be true or not to be true?'

'Listening at the drawing-room door, wasn't I?'

'Vilkins, dear.'

'Oh, come on, Unwin, a girl's got to protec' 'erself in this life, ain't she? An' got to look arter 'er friends too.'

Miss Unwin smiled.

'Well, dear, I must confess I am glad you did do what you did to look after me. I am certainly in trouble again. Worse trouble, I somehow think, than I was in before.'

'Oh, yes,' Vilkins agreed promptly. 'You are worse now, Unwin. A 'ole lot worse, if you ask me. You see, before this you knew what it was what poisoned the old man an' all you 'ad to do was go about looking till you found someone as 'ad it. But now . . . Now you don't even know so much as what to look for.'

Miss Unwin sighed.

Vilkins had done her exercise in logic for her, and had done it well. There might be other complications she had to think out, but the main difficulty that confronted her had been put fair and squarely before her.

163

'Yes, you're right,' she said. 'And – And, well, dear, you know my secret. So I am still faced with trying to make Inspector Redderman look further than his nose.'

'Yeh. I 'eard that bit, too, just afore I made meself scarce. 'Im an' 'is answer that provides fewest difficulties. That was it, wasn't it?'

'Yes. Yes, it was. In some ways, though, I hardly blame him. He knows old Mr Partington was poisoned, and he has to ask himself who had most to gain by his death. Well, it's clear who that is, and there is nothing Richard – nothing Mr Partington can do to prove beyond doubt that he is not the person responsible. So in a way the Inspector is right to think as he does.'

'Well,' Vilkins said, 'I s'pose 'e may 'ave got the correc' answer too.'

'No, Vilkins. No.'

'Well, all right, all right. But you said it yourself, there's nothing your Richard's been able to do to prove as 'ow 'e ain't the one.'

'No. No, I know that you are right in logic, and I must bear the thought as well as I may. But, surely, surely, someone else who could possibly have given the poison, whatever it is, must have done so.'

'Well, there's that old devil over Ratcliff 'Ighway. Or is she off the 'ook now?'

'Because it wasn't arsenic that was the poison? Well, I suppose that does make it a lot less likely that Mrs Meggs is to blame. But it is still possible she was the one who gave him whatever other poison it was.'

'But she wouldn't of found it so easy to get 'old of something else, would she?'

'No, I imagine she would not, though we don't really know till Professor Potherton has found out just what the poison was.'

'An' 'ow long's 'e going to be over that? What's 'e do? Smell it or something?'

'I don't exactly know, dear. There are dozens and

dozens of tests for various substances, or so I gathered from the professor's own book.'

'An' I don't suppose anybody'll be good enough to tell us when they do know,' Vilkins said in her gloomiest tone.

'No, you're right again there. So what am I to do?'

'Well, there's always that Captain Fulcher you were so keen on 'aving strung up for the job.'

'Oh, Vilkins, don't say that. I'm not anxious to see anybody hanged. But – But –'

'But you're a bit less keen on seeing your Richard on the end of a rope than someone else, ain't you?'

'Yes. Yes, I am.'

'Then who do you want to see there?'

'Who do I think is most likely to have done the thing that they deserve to be hanged for? I suppose Captain Fulcher, as you say. But my efforts there came to precious little.'

'Well, what about that sister of 'is then?'

'I know so little about the life she led here in London,' Miss Unwin answered. 'I don't know whether she would have been able to obtain a poison, any poison, whatever poison was used.'

She sighed.

'But you can find out, can't you?' said Vilkins.

'Yes,' said Miss Unwin. 'Yes, at least I can do that, or try to do it. To find out about Miss Cornelia Fulcher's life up here in London when she was letting all the world believe she was down in the West Country.'

She felt a surge of hope, a quick running of the blood.

'Yes, but 'ow you going to do that, Unwin?'

Miss Unwin's eyes shone with the light of battle.

'By having a good long talk with that little servant girl in the house in Great Marlborough Street,' she said. 'You remember I told you about her?'

'Cheeky little beggar, by all accounts.'

'Yes. And all the more ready to tell secrets she should not.'

'So when you going to go? An' can I come with you?'

'Tomorrow,' said Miss Unwin. 'Tomorrow morning, and of course we'll go together.'

Then she remembered.

'Oh, but the twins. I cannot let them go once more without their lessons.'

'But you'll 'ave to, won't you?' said Vilkins.

With sinking heart Miss Unwin assented.

Perhaps once more would not matter. Perhaps just one more morning away from her duties would not result in the girls, already spoiled enough, getting up to worse mischief. And one more absence might be all she needed. With some good evidence that Miss Cornelia Fulcher had made some attempt to acquire some poison or other she could, yet again, go to Inspector Redderman. And this time the case she presented would be the one that in the end would stick.

Next day all her hopes seemed to be being rewarded. The twins, when she had given them each one of Mrs Molesworth's books to read, a pleasant occupation she thought, made no difficulties about being left on their own once again. Mrs Miller in her kitchen was quite happy to let Vilkins go out on a carefully unspecified errand. And when they reached the house in Great Marlborough Street the slatternly little girl of the establishment was outside on the step, scrubbing at it with a block of holystone in no very industrious way.

Miss Unwin placed Vilkins in the background and boldly tackled the girl.

'Do you want to earn half a crown?'

The girl looked at her with patent suspicion.

'I seen you afore.'

'Yes, you have. And you told me a little about your lodgers then. I want to know more now. Do you want that half-crown?'

'I want three shillin'.'

'You shall have them.'

'First?'

Miss Unwin took a florin from her purse.

'The last shilling comes when you have told me as much as you know.'

The girl stood sulkily considering.

'What yer want ter know then?'

'Everything you can tell me about Miss Fulcher. What she does with her days. Where she goes shopping. What she buys. What she has bought and keeps in the rooms. That will do to begin with.'

'Then I'll 'ave ter 'ave another florin. An' straight-away.'

Miss Unwin longed to box the wretched creature's ears.

'Not a penny more until I hear what I want to hear,' she said.

The girl smirked.

'Yer won't learn noffink wivout what I tells yer,' she said. 'An' I won't tell wivout me money.'

'You'll get your money, another two shillings if you like, when you have given me your information.'

'No,' said the girl. 'An' yer needn't think you'll get anyfing out o' old Mr Bessom either. Too drunk ter tell yer. Never out o' the Grapes over Seven Dials, 'e ain't.'

Miss Unwin felt a dart of impatience. Had the luck which had been with her all morning run out? If this snot-nosed creature delayed telling her what she wanted much longer it was quite possible Mrs Bessom would emerge from the house to see why her girl was being so long over cleaning the step.

But to yield to her blackmailing would be only to give the creature the chance of making new demands.

'You will tell me what I want, or you will see me no more.'

'I'll keep yer ruddy florin then.'

'But you'll get no other.'

167

'Oh, orright then. If yer must.'

'Well now, tell me: Miss Fulcher, does she go out shopping every day?'

'Nah. Too mean.'

'Does she never go out then?'

'Yeh. Sometimes.'

'To the shops? Do you know which ones?'

'She goes to the oilman's. Buys fly papers by the dozen. Silly cow.'

Fly papers. Miss Unwin's interest leapt up for one instant. But the arsenic in fly papers was not what had poisoned old Mr Partington.

'What else does she buy?'

'Dunno. Goes ter the chemist. Always a-coming back wiv little bottles wrapped up in white paper an' sealed wi' wax.'

'Does she? And what is in those packets?'

The girl's eyes took on a look of fierce cunning.

'Dunno, do I?'

'I think you know very well. Don't tell me you don't poke and pry in Miss Fulcher's bedroom when you go in to sweep.'

'What if I do? You ain't going ter tell on me, are yer?'

Miss Unwin very much would have liked to have gone straight into the house and told Mrs Bessom just what her maidservant did. But the girl was right. She was not going to 'tell on her.'

'Never mind telling. What is it that Miss Fulcher buys in those packets from the chemist?'

The girl considered. Doubtless she was debating whether this was the moment to raise the bidding.

But she had left it too late.

The door behind her was jerked suddenly back and in the doorway stood a woman who could only be Mrs Bessom, a broad, formidable figure, red-faced and beetle-browed beneath a wide-frilled white cap jammed on her head with the force of a steam-hammer.

She took one look at Miss Unwin.
'And what may you be wanting?' she demanded.

Chapter Seventeen

Miss Unwin was at a loss for an answer to the barked-out question the Fulchers' landlady had challenged her with. Or she was so for more long moments than she cared to think about. But at last the resources of her mind produced something.

'Good morning,' she said, forcing a cool tone on to herself. 'I am afraid I strayed from Oxford Street and am now quite lost. I thought to inquire from your girl here, and somehow, I know not how, we fell into conversation. I am sorry if I kept her from her work.'

She had said too much, and she knew it. But she had provided herself with a path of retreat and this she took.

Not until she was in the bustle of Oxford Street did she stop to discuss with Vilkins the sudden defeat of a campaign that had seemed to be going so well.

'Oh, Vilkins, Vilkins, so near and yet so far.'

'Yeh. Fancy coming out an' spying on the girl. I wouldn't stand for it meself.'

'Well, I dare say you would lose your place if you behaved as badly as that creature.'

'Yeh. I'm surprised she ain't been thrown out on 'er ear long ago.'

'Ah, I think I know the reason for that. Mrs Bessom, fierce though she looks, must like to leave that sort of thing to her husband. And Mr Bessom is a weak man.'

'In that gin palace at Seven Dials,' said Vilkins knowingly.

'Yes, the Grapes, didn't the girl say? Do you know of it then.'

171

'In course I do. As rough a place as there is going. But the gin's cheap, if you can stand the company.'

And it was then that a terrible idea came into Miss Unwin's mind.

'Vilkins,' she said, 'I think that I must visit the Grapes.'

'Visit the Grapes? Unwin, you gone off your nut?'

'No. No, I know it is an insane proposition in many ways. But, don't you see, in the Grapes I could meet Mr Bessom. And Mr Bessom, I dare swear, would tell me everything that little girl was going to.'

'You're right there, I should think. Lazy layabout like 'im he'd 'ave nothing better to do than poke 'is nose into the lodgers' business.'

'So you see, dear, rough though Seven Dials is, I must make my way there and take a drink at the Grapes, come what may.'

'You'll do nothing o' the sort.'

'But I must, Vilkins, I must. Little though I relish the idea.'

'You'll do nothing o' the sort. But I will. An' that's all there is to be said about it. You, if you went in one o' them ginshops down Seven Dials, you wouldn't last ten minutes. Not five. But I'd be all right. I kept to the rough, didn't I? I wouldn't go too far wrong down the Grapes.'

'No, Vilkins.'

'Yes, Unwin.'

'But why should you do this for me? I am the one who wants to find a case against someone other than Richard Partington. It cannot mean much to you.'

'It don't mean nothing. Not 'im.'

'Then you shall not go.'

'He don't mean nothing to me. Why should 'e? Ain't seen all that much of 'im, 'ave I? But you mean something to me, Unwin. You mean a 'ell of a lot to me. You're the only friend what I ever 'ad.'

And, though there was more argument, Miss Unwin knew that with those words she was going to let Vilkins

172

venture into Seven Dials and rely on her to find out at the Grapes from weak Mr Bessom what it was that Cornelia Fulcher bought at the chemist's shop.

But when after Vilkins had served dinner that evening – she spilt nothing, a rare occurrence – she came to Miss Unwin's room dressed once more in her garish bonnet it was with a mind full of misgivings that Miss Unwin let her go.

'You won't – Vilkins, dear, you won't let anyone . . .'

'Don't you worry your 'ead,' Vilkins said. 'I'd like to see the man what thinks 'e can 'ave 'is way with me.'

'Well, dear, I hope you're right. And you've got the cab money safe?'

'Tucked in me garter. An' there ain't no one going to get at it there.'

But nevertheless, even before the earliest time it was likely that her friend could have completed her errand at the Grapes Miss Unwin was fidgeting and waiting for her, glancing through the curtains of her window every two or three minutes hard though she tried to stop herself.

It was for this reason that the sounds coming from the landing took some time to impinge on her consciousness.

The children, she thought at once, when the little scuffling noises she had heard without hearing finally came to that forefront of her mind. Surely they cannot be doing again what they did the night I found out about old Mr Partington's hoard?

Nevertheless she kicked off her shoes – she was still fully dressed, ready to welcome Vilkins on her return – and hurried out to look into the twins' room. And those two new white beds with the pink-knotted curtains were empty.

Miss Unwin ran downstairs.

What were the girls doing? Surely now, when their father was giving them all and more that they could wish for, they were not setting out to steal once again? Grave though their fault was when they had attempted to take

173

one of the sovereigns in the hoard they had discovered, it was something that could be understood of children who had never been allowed into a sweetshop. But now . . .? Could they really be stealing once more?

In the hall they were nowhere to be seen. Miss Unwin, grim faced, set out for the basement and the kitchen.

And, as she crept down the stairs, there where it should have been pitch dark she saw the glow of candlelight.

But what could the girls be wanting down in the basement? Their grandfather's gold had long ago been taken away. And they could hardly want anything from the larder. The meals they ate now were so large that it was a wonder they did not become ill. Let alone the sweets their father kept offering them now he was home again.

Soft-footed and cautious, Miss Unwin peered round the corner at the foot of the stairs towards the clearer glow of the candle.

And, facing her, on tip-toe, with secret intent looks, there were Louisa and Maria. Maria was holding the candle, not the guttering stub of that earlier expedition but a tall white candle in a pretty china candlestick from their bedroom. And Louisa had in the cupped palm of her hand something she was at pains to keep from spilling.

'Girls!'

Louisa screamed and from her hand there fell a stream of bright yellow powder. The candle in Maria's hand wavered dangerously.

'Give me that,' Miss Unwin said, stepping forward and grasping the pretty china stick before the candle set the whole house on fire.

She turned to Louisa.

'And what is that that you have got there?'

'Nothing, Miss.'

'Don't be silly, Louisa. It is not nothing. What is it?'

'It – It really is nothing. I mean, it is of no consequence.'

'Leave me to be the judge of consequence. What is it

174

that you have there? I will not ask you again.'

'Then don't, Miss.'

Louisa's face was a study in sullen mutinousness.

Miss Unwin put down the candle and took the girl's wrist firmly in her hand. She brought the clenched fist up closely to her nose.

'Mustard,' she said. 'You have got a handful of mustard powder there. What on earth are you doing?'

'Nothing, Miss.'

'Nothing? What has got into you tonight? I come down here when I find you out of your beds and I catch you clutching a handful of mustard. You cannot tell me then that you are doing nothing.'

Louisa stood in silence.

'Maria, what were you doing?'

But before Maria could answer, her sister flashed her a look which said plainly as if it were written out, *Say nothing*.

'We weren't doing anything, Miss Unwin.'

'Maria, I expected better things of you. Coming down to the kitchen and possessing yourselves of mustard is not doing nothing. Now, what is all this about?'

But, under Louisa's baleful stare, Maria, too, was now silent.

Miss Unwin looked at the pair of them. This was altogether unusual behaviour. Certainly, when she had first come to the house neither girl was at all ladylike in manner. But they had quite soon become responsive to what she said and before very long they had learnt too, to obey. Yet now . . . This rebellious muteness. It was altogether new.

She sighed.

'Very well. Go up to your beds now, and go straight to sleep. Not one word to each other, understand. And in the morning we will talk about this again.'

Severe as a prison wardress, she escorted them back to

their room, saw them into bed, extinguished their candle and waited outside until she was happy that no further rebellion was contemplated.

Then she went back to her own room.

And saw the clock.

It was late, very late, and Vilkins had not returned from dangerous Seven Dials.

She should never have let her go. Especially not on her own.

All that she had ever heard about the notorious Rookery at St Giles, of which Seven Dials with its seven converging streets and seven roaring gin palaces was the centre, came back into her head. There were thieves to be seen there of every sort, safe from the police who ventured into the area only in bands and who, when they did make a capture, were likely to hear the cry of 'Rescue' and find themselves assaulted by a mob. There, drinking where Vilkins had undertaken to find weak-willed Mr Bessom, were the bludgers who would think nothing of beating anyone of obvious wealth into insensibility and the broadsmen, less cruel but tenacious of their gains at faked card games and all too ready to spend them on any girl who took their fancy. Or there were the flimps, slipping adroit fingers into pockets and purses, and the pudding snammers, stealing from careless people coming out of cookshops. Would one of these take, by force or cunning, the small, hard-earned sum she had given Vilkins as cab fare?

Or was Vilkins coming safely home in a cab even now? It was late enough to have justified the spending of some of that diminishing amount of her savings. Or was she out of foolish kindness coming home by omnibus?

But was she coming back at all? And, if she was, had she found Mr Bessom? And had she succeeded in worming out of him what he knew about Cousin Cornelia and her visits to the chemist's shop? Was there even, after all, nothing sinister in those visits?

And how late it was.

Was Vilkins even at this moment in some vile nethersken on a broken-down bed at the mercy of some bully or other?

She should never have allowed her to make that offer out of their long friendship.

And here at home, what was it that Louisa had been up to? Stealing mustard from the kitchen? What could be her purpose? And in the morning when she and Maria were asked again, would they tell?

The night wore on. The whole household was asleep now, and had been for some hours. Miss Unwin had long ago blown out her candle. But, though the night was chill, she kept her window open the better to look out for the first sign of her friend, the better to hear in the night-time silence at the edge of the great city the sound of a cab-horse's hooves clacking out on the cobbles, or even Vilkins' sturdy boots clumping wearily along the last stretch of the long walk home.

Chapter Eighteen

But when at last the faint whitening of the sky through Miss Unwin's window indicated that the new day was coming Vilkins had still not returned. Miss Unwin was in despair. She had made up her mind that at some moment she would have to go and see Inspector Redderman and tell him just what she had done, how she had allowed Vilkins to go on that ridiculous and dangerous errand. She would have to throw herself on the Inspector's mercy and beg him to ask his fellow policemen at the station house near the Rookery to raid the area.

But, even if the Inspector would consent to that, she knew that the chances of finding Vilkins in the Rookery with its scores of underground passages linking one tumbledown house with another, with its specially contrived escape ways over roofs and along the tops of walls, were slim indeed. Vilkins could be being held by some desperate man who had taken a fancy to her, and no one would know for weeks or months where she was. She could have been murdered and it would be long, long, if ever, before her body was found.

But though she had made up her mind that Inspector Redderman sooner or later would have to be told, she could not decide at what precise moment it would be best to give him the news. It was possible that, even at this dawn hour, Vilkins would return. It was worth waiting still.

Then, early though it was, she heard the twins talking in their room. Another problem.

She resolved at least to deal with that. Perhaps by the

time she had learnt what on earth it was that had possessed them to steal mustard from the larder and what they had intended to do with their prize, Vilkins would have returned and her other dilemma be ended.

But the moment she entered the girls' room she knew she was to be faced with a stiff battle. They had each fallen abruptly silent, and now they gave one another quick glances of complicity before, sitting up in their beds with the curtains pulled back, they began looking with studious care at the story books they had on the tables beside them.

'You can put away those books,' Miss Unwin said drily. 'And I shall not ask you to tell me what you have been reading in them.'

She half-expected Louisa to ask impertinently why not. But the girl said not a word and let her book fall closed on the bedclothes in front of her. Maria, more tidily, shut her volume with care and placed it on her table.

'Now,' Miss Unwin said, 'when we last saw each other you were clutching a handful of mustard powder, Louisa. Why was that?'

'I just was, Miss.'

'No, that will not do. What had you taken the mustard from the larder for?'

'We just thought it would be a good idea.'

'Well, it was not. Maria, can you give me a better answer than your sister?'

'No, Miss Unwin.'

'Come, Maria, you're a sensible girl. You cannot think I will believe you when you say you "just did" take the mustard. Tell me why you did, and perhaps we will hear no more about it.'

'She has told you, Miss Unwin,' Louisa said quickly.

'No, Louisa, she has not. And neither have you. And what is more when I ask Maria something I will thank you not to answer for her.'

'Yes, Miss,' Louisa replied, with great humility.

Miss Unwin felt a dart of anger. But she suppressed it.

'Now, Maria, I will ask you once again. Why were you two down in the larder in the middle of the night taking mustard powder?'

'Don't know, Miss.'

'Oh, come, Maria.'

Silence.

'Maria, this is your very last chance. Now, why did you two take that mustard?'

And Maria, who Miss Unwin had hoped would prove the weaker vessel, once more stayed silent, though she hung her head and blushed a deep and anxious red.

Miss Unwin sighed.

'Very well,' she said, 'since you are both so obstinate you will have to be punished.'

Maria then did give her a half-glance in which there was a good measure of fear.

She waited hopefully. At the last moment would the girl break? Would she reveal a secret which, with every passing minute it seemed, might be connected with that greater, looming, more terrible secret under which the whole house had lain ever since old Mr Partington's death?

But if Louisa, the leader, did not flagrantly disobey the injunction not to answer on behalf of her twin, she nevertheless managed by as little as a single twitch of her blankets to convey a warning. And Maria took it in, hung her head again, hunched her shoulders in obstinacy and said not a word.

'Very well. Now you will both get dressed in silence. Then you, Louisa, will go to the schoolroom and you will remain there all day. You, Maria, will stay in here. And all either of you will get to eat will be bread and water.'

'Yes, Miss.'

'Yes, Miss.'

Miss Unwin watched the two girls in silence while they dressed and washed. Then she escorted Louisa to the schoolroom and left her there.

But she was not happy as she went downstairs. She had hoped that in the time she had been the girls' governess she had won their confidence. They ought to have yielded to the pressures she had put on them to confess their misdemeanour. But they had not. She felt she had failed as an instructress. And, worse, she feared that the girls' obstinacy meant it was no trivial misdemeanour they had committed, or had been beginning to commit, when she had surprised them down in the basement.

Well, she would have to tell their father of the steps she had taken when she met him at the breakfast table. And where was Vilkins?

Although it wanted some minutes to the breakfast hour Miss Unwin made her way towards the dining room since, with the twins confined, she had no immediate task.

Just as she was about to open the door she heard a sound. For a moment she paused. Then she took in what it was. The sound of the breakfast cutlery being put in place. With more than a little noisy clumsiness. Vilkins.

She flung the door open, hastily closed it behind her.

'Vilkins, how did you get here? When did you come?'

'Oh, lawks, Unwin, I 'ad such a time an' all. Only just got to the 'ouse five minutes ago, an' Mrs Miller looking for me high an' low.'

'Yes, I ought to have gone down and warned her you were not here, but I had some trouble with the girls.'

'Good thing you didn't say nothing. I told 'er I just slipped out to post a letter. Not that I've ever done such a thing as write a letter in me life, only she ain't to know that, is she?'

'No, I suppose not. But, Vilkins, what kept you? What happened to you? Are you all right?'

'Well, all right I am. More or less. Scraped me leg

182

something terrible getting off of the omnibus this morning. Driver wouldn't stop in course, weren't no toffs on board.'

Miss Unwin knew well that few bus drivers did more than slow their horses to a walk if their passengers were not from among the gentry. But she had more urgent business than commiserating with Vilkins over her injury, which hardly seemed to prevent her in any case from banging rapidly round the table.

'But, Vilkins, why were you out all night? Let me know.'

'Well, it's a long story.'

Vilkins glanced at the dining-room door.

'But it wants nearly ten minutes till breakfast time. Tell me, Vilkins, tell me. First, were you in danger?'

'Danger? Well, I' s'pose I was in a way. But I got out of it in the end with me skin 'ole.'

'Thank goodness that you did. Thank goodness. I would never have forgiven –'

And then, behind her, she heard the door briskly opened.

She turned.

It was Richard. Richard, looking well and spruce, dressed in one of his best new coats, so different from the turned garment that until not so long ago had been the only coat he possessed.

He had been smiling when he had entered, a broad grin that lit his whole round face. But at the sight of Vilkins he checked.

'Ah. Ah, Mary, it's you. Good morning.'

''Morning, sir.'

'Mary, I wonder if you would leave us for a few minutes.'

'Well, I has got to get the table laid. An' I'm all behindhand this morning.'

'Yes, well, never mind. We can breakfast a little late and no harm done.'

183

'Well, I dunno what Mrs M will say. Stickler for getting 'er bacon just so, she is.'

Miss Unwin thought it high time to intervene.

'I'll say a word to Cook, Mary,' she said. 'Do go along now.'

'All right. Never said I wasn't going, did I?'

She trailed off.

'I'm not so sure about your recommendation of that girl,' Richard said. 'But never mind about that now. I've – I've something much more important to say.'

For a moment Miss Unwin wondered whether there and then before breakfast the impetuous man she loved was going to put to her in form the proposal he had been prevented from making before.

But even Richard was not quite such a dashing lover.

'Harriet,' he said, 'I thought of this in the middle of the night. Now, listen. This evening, will you come down with me to Greenwich, on one of the boats and dine with me at the Trafalgar Inn. It's – It's something I've always wanted to do, and of course –'

He came to a full stop.

'Well,' he went on, 'it has never been possible before. So, Harriet, will you? Will you? Say you will.'

Miss Unwin knew well that it was more than a trip down the river and a fine dinner at Greenwich that Richard was offering her. She saw at once that at that dinner, or perhaps immediately after it, he was intending to put the question to her that would change her whole life. And though, before, she had felt some inner, indefinable unwillingness to accept that which with all her heart she thought she was willing to accept, now with the flood of relief at Vilkins' safety strong within her she did not hesitate for a moment.

'Well, sir, if you wish me to go down to Greenwich with you, I will, with the greatest pleasure.'

Then, feeling it very much to be a cloud on an azure sea of happiness, she felt obliged to tell Richard about the

184

unusual misbehaviour of his daughters and what she had had to do about it.

'Oh, dear. Oh, dear. Oh, dear. Well, this does mar the occasion. But you did quite right. You did quite right indeed, though I doubt if I would have managed to be as stern. No. As just. Yes, I doubt if I would have managed to be as just myself.'

'Well, sir, we must hope that they repent before very long. Then, though they will not eat a fine Greenwich dinner, we can ask Cook to give them something special to make up for their hard regime.'

'Yes. Yes, we'll do that. And perhaps another box of those sugar-plums they like so much.'

'Well, you are indulgent, sir. But I suppose occasional indulgence is not too bad a thing.'

But even as she spoke Miss Unwin realised what the mustard that the twins had been so secretive about had been intended for. The box of sugar-plums she had taken from them. They must have been meaning, when she had let them have them again, to fill each plum and then to offer it to – To herself as a little revenge? Or to their father as a prank?

Well, in either case, though it was a piece of naughtiness which ought to meet with a rebuke, it was not something that was as serious as she had feared.

But this was no time to think about a trivial piece of mischief. There was more, much more, to think about. There was the evening that was to lie ahead, a trip down the broad flowing Thames by steamer – thank goodness the day was fine and promised to stay so – and then dinner in one of the big inns overlooking the river with perhaps the moon shining on its tranquil waters. And then . . . And then Richard to say something to her, to say words that once she had thought she might never hear said. And then . . .

After that, mistiness. Let what would happen after those words had been spoken, that question asked,

185

remain at least for the present deliciously unknown.

But more. There was Vilkins still to think of. How wonderful that all those fears of the night had been banished. What trouble Vilkins had got into and got out of she had still to learn. But it was a trouble that, it was plain, had been got out of without anything impossible to contemplate having happened. Vilkins' cheerful, and not very respectful, answers to her master over leaving the breakfast half-laid showed that.

And had Vilkins learnt something about Miss Fulcher that would lift the cloud hanging over this house for ever? It would be very much like Vilkins not to have arranged her thoughts enough to have put that vital piece of business to the forefront. So it might yet be there to be told. Good news.

There came a knock, or rather thump, at the door.

'Come in,' Miss Unwin called.

Vilkins reappeared with her tray.

'Can I get on with it now?'

'Yes. Yes, Mary, of course.'

How exasperating to have Vilkins there before her eyes and, with Richard present, not to be able to ask her a single question. But it would not be long till breakfast was over and there could be contrived an opportunity for a few minutes' private talk with her old friend.

Chapter Nineteen

Miss Unwin decided that it would be sufficient punishment for the twins to let them stay in their separate rooms until breakfast was over. One meal of bread and water, not so different from the breakfasts they had had up to the time their grandfather had been poisoned, would be a reminder to them of what they now had and stood to lose.

So, even before contriving her talk in private with Vilkins, she went up to the girls' bedroom, took Maria with her to the schoolroom and there confronted them both with what she had guessed.

'You wanted to put mustard into the sugar-plums I took away from you, didn't you?'

She let her gaze, severe as she could make it, rest equally on both culprits.

Maria broke first. She gave her sister only the most fleeting of glances by way of obtaining permission to break a sworn compact. Then, with evident relief, she spoke.

'Yes, Miss. Yes. Was it very bad of us?'

'Well, it was not the sort of behaviour I should have expected. Was it, Louisa?'

'No, Miss. But I don't think we'd have put very much in the plums.'

'I'm glad to hear it. And let me hear, too, that you will, neither of you, contemplate doing such a thing again.'

'Oh, no, Miss Unwin, we never will.'

'Louisa?'

'No, we won't. We won't contemplate filling sugar-plums with mustard ever, ever again.'

'Very well. Then we will begin lessons in half an hour.'

'Miss Unwin?'

'Yes, Louisa?'

'Can we have our proper breakfast now?'

'No, Louisa, you most certainly cannot.'

So Miss Unwin went in search of Vilkins and her account of what she had done and what she had found out in St Giles' Rookery. Yet, even as she went, a faint tingling of doubt manifested itself in her mind. Had the girls been a little too quick to confess to their misdemeanour? Had she herself made a mistake in, with the welling-up of happiness she felt, telling them what she believed they had done instead of getting them to tell her first?

She shook her head.

This was not a day for doubts. This was, was to be, a day of unimaginable happiness when towards its close down at Greenwich a certain question was to be asked, a question which she knew her answer to. And, more immediately, Vilkins might really have, somewhere in the cheerful muddle of her mind, the answer to the mystery that still hung over them all.

If before the day was done the cloud of suspicion had been finally and irrevocably lifted from Richard, and if Richard had asked her – had asked her a certain question, then what a day of rejoicing it would prove to have been.

'Vilkins.'

Vilkins was down on her hands and knees, her rump in the air, brushing at the carpet newly laid outside the dining room. Miss Unwin opened the door behind her. The dining room was empty, Richard having drunk his last cup of tea, eaten his last muffin.

'Come in here quickly, my dear, and tell me all about everything.'

'Unwin, I can't. I'm all behind with me work.'

Miss Unwin had not used a single oath since the day she had been released from the workhouse to go as a

188

kitchen-maid, the start of her path upwards in the world. But at this moment she nearly said 'Damn your work.'

Instead she bent down, seized poor Vilkins by the arm and unceremoniously dragged her into the temporary privacy of the dining room.

'Now, just what happened at St Giles?'

'I was chased.'

'Chased? Who by?'

'Great 'ulking mulatto. Took a fancy to me in the Grapes, 'e did. Lickin' 'is lips from right acrost the room.'

'And you had to leave to get rid of him?'

Miss Unwin would by far have preferred to be hearing whether Vilkins had found Mr Bessom and whether that weak-willed lodgings owner knew why Miss Cornelia Fulcher visited the chemist's shop and what was in the well-wrapped bottles she brought back. But she felt she owed it to Vilkins, who had so willingly risked so much out of mere friendship, to hear her adventures as she wanted to tell them.

'Yeh,' Vilkins answered, cheerfully enough. ''Ad to lead 'im a merry dance, I did. An' nearly got caught more times than I likes to remember. Nip along an alley I would, thinking I'd thrown 'im off once an' for all, an' what should I see at the far end? The man hisself. Could 'e run. Must be the fastest man in England, if 'e was only a Englishman.'

'But he never did catch you?'

'Oh, yes, 'e did.'

'Oh, Vilkins. But what – What happened?'

'Took a liberty, 'e did. There was I up against a wall, an' 'im with 'is great black arms either side o' me. Then 'e took a liberty.'

Miss Unwin looked at her friend.

'What liberty?' she asked.

'He kissed me. Kissed me right on the end o' me nose.'

Miss Unwin suppressed a laugh. This was a day for happiness.

189

'But, Vilkins, that wasn't too bad,' she said.

A grin spread itself round Vilkins' face.

'Wasn't too bad, considerin' what I did to 'im arter,' she said.

'Oh, Vilkins, what?'

'Bit 'is bleedin' nose back I did. 'E was so surprised 'e clapped 'is great big 'ands to it, an' I got clean away. Only I was lost then, an' couldn't find me way out till I got a bit o' daylight.'

'And then you found an omnibus and came home, safe all but for a scraped shin getting down, wasn't it? But, Vilkins, why didn't you take a cab home? You had enough money, hadn't you?

'Well, I ought to 'ave 'ad. But I didn't take account of Mr Bessom an' the way 'e can sink the gin.'

'Oh, Vilkins, you had to stand him so much liquor that you spent all that money?'

'That's right. But it was worth it.'

'Worth it? What did you find out from him then? What? What?'

'Monkshood,' said Vilkins. 'That's what I found out. Monkshood.'

'Monkshood? What's that, my dear?'

'Poison,' said Vilkins in fittingly sepulchral tones.

'What? You mean that Miss Fulcher was buying monkshood and that that is some sort of poison?'

Miss Unwin went rapidly over in her mind what she had read in *Potherton on Poisons*. But she could not recall any reference to monkshood. Had Vilkins got it wrong? It was, alas, all too possible.

'What exactly did Mr Bessom tell you about this monkshood that Miss Fulcher is said to have bought?'

'Ain't no "said to" about it. Bought it she did, by the bottle. An' poison it is. Everyone knows that.'

Miss Unwin noted that, for once, her friend apparently knew more than she did. And she was inclined to believe her. If Vilkins said everyone knew something, there could be little doubt that a good number of people did know. In which case monkshood – that was presumably the popular name – was something fatal to anyone who had it administered to them.

'Did Mr Bessom see what Miss Fulcher did with the monkshood?' she asked.

'No. Couldn't find out nothing. An', don't you see, that makes it all the more likely she was a-giving it to the poor old gentleman? If she was so secret, stands to reason it was something wicked, don't it?'

Miss Unwin found herself inclined to think her friend's reasoning might be sound.

She made up her mind in a moment. She would set the twins a task which she could sit and watch them at, and then she would take *Potherton on Poisons* once more and comb through it till she found a reference to monkshood. If it was only a country name, it was understandable that she did not recall it. Professor Potherton was not a man to make use of popular names. The Latin language was his preferred territory.

'Well, I'll leave you to get on with your work, dear,' she said to Vilkins. 'And I had better return to mine.'

'If you can call looking arter a pair o' kiddies work,' said Vilkins, dropping to her knees on the carpet once more.

Well, Miss Unwin thought, as with the two girls confronting Butter's *Spelling* she settled down to Professor Potherton, I certainly do call this work. And it is work which I devoutly hope will bring great gains.

To Richard. To Richard.

And within a quarter of an hour gain her reading had brought.

Monkshood, Professor Potherton deigned to mention, was the popular name for acontine, known also as wolfsbane 'and to the Ancient Greeks by the nomenclature Stepmother's Poison.'

For a moment Miss Unwin's heart raced with excitement. Had she at last found out how old Mr

Partington had perished: Had she found his murderess? Acontine, she read, was a poison that it was not possible to detect except by a judicious tasting of extract from the tissues most immediately affected, 'a proceeding of extreme hazardousness'. So no wonder the professor's findings were so delayed.

Eagerly she read on.

And almost at once encountered defeat. 'Aconitia,' Professor Potherton wrote, 'though of some medical use as a liniment for the relief of rheumatism and neuralgia, is particularly to be noted for the speed and violence of its onset if imbibed. Few survive more than a few minutes.'

But Mr Partington had survived many hours. He had, indeed, it seemed most likely, survived more than one dose.

So whatever had poisoned him, it was not after all monkshood. And Cousin Cornelia was not the murderess, merely most probably a sufferer from neuralgia.

It was all to be looked at again. Her heart sank.

She gave a great sigh and slammed *Potherton on Poisons* shut.

'Now, girls,' she said, 'let us see if you can spell every word in your lists without error.'

So the day that was to be the great day of happiness wore on, with one blight cast on its perfection. Miss Unwin tried not to think about that. But she could not prevent herself being conscious that the day was not what she had once thought it was to be.

In the late afternoon she found herself setting out for the Greenwich steamer with Richard. The hours since she had tested the twins' spelling – only Louisa got one of Butter's list wrong, and Miss Unwin contrived not to hear her error – had gone by in busy affairs of one sort or another. She had not had time to begin to think again who could have murdered old Mr Partington if Miss Fulcher had not. Was it after all her brother, hoping to hide some misappropriation of hidden sovereigns? Or was it Mrs

Meggs, wanting what she had been told she was to get in the Will? Or was it some other unthinkable alternative?

Neither had she time to consider the final object of the expedition to Greenwich, to wonder at what precise moment Richard planned to ask the all important question. She had not even had time to think about how she would give her answer.

In the cab on the way to the pier at London Bridge Richard was jolly and jocose. Plainly this was not the hour he had chosen. So she succumbed to his mood. What she had to consider if she let her mind dwell on serious matters was so difficult, so forbidding, that she snatched at the opportunity to postpone hard thought.

As they boarded the steamer Richard's high spirits became yet more ebullient. Everything he saw seemed to provide subject for a joke or a fantastic story. A police cutter rowed by at speed, its oarsmen flashing their blades to a steady rhythm.

'You know why that's called a cutter?'

'Because it cuts through the water at such a pace, surely.'

'Quite wrong. It's because that sort of boat was invented at Calcutta in India, and the word has become somewhat corrupted.'

'Oh, Richard. Such tarradiddles. What an example to the girls.'

'But the girls are not here to be set an example.'

For a moment then Miss Unwin thought that it had entered Richard's mind to say what had to be said without the presence of the twins. But the moment passed.

And she was glad. Because in those two seconds in which the question might have been broached the thought had come to her that while there loomed over Richard the faintest shadow of Inspector Redderman's suspicions she would not be able to answer with the fervant 'Yes' which her whole being seemed to be on the point of crying out.

But that was a matter of a few moments only. For all the

rest of their voyage down the river light-heartedness reigned. In her mind as plainly as it did in Richard's.

With steadily churning paddle-wheels they chuffed their way between the tall warehouses on either bank. They passed the grim old bastion of the Tower. They watched the anchored shipping slip by. They speculated on what business was taking lone rowers in little wherries hither and thither. They wondered what tales a tall Indiaman, its masts silhouetted against the evening sky, might tell.

Time slipped by.

And then they had arrived, and Richard had swept her into the private room he had telegraphed for at the Trafalgar, a room with a balcony overlooking the swirling river.

And she had protested.

'Richard, a private room. It must cost so much. And to have telegraphed to order it. You – You must not –'

Then she checked herself. Not over what Richard must or must not do, but over what she must not do. She must not anticipate a wifely right to forbid or advise against a husband's actions.

'What must I not do?'

'Oh, nothing, nothing. I spoke without thinking.'

Then the meal that Richard had ordered was served, and with it a great magnum of champagne.

Once again Miss Unwin nearly forbade the man she loved doing something. He, who had had almost as little opportunity as herself to drink wine, must not, she had almost said, even with her assistance drink so much. But this time she succeeded in keeping quite silent, though she felt a tiny sinking at having wished to speak.

Indeed, as the dinner unrolled its huge length, she was tempted more than once to rebuke the man who she knew was, at its termination, going to ask her to be his wife. Even the thought that she was now fully determined to postpone her answer until she and the whole world was aware who had poisoned Richard's father did not make the temptation any less to speak out about his wild extravagance.

But at the turtle soup, rich and rare, she refrained. When vol au vents and cold salmon were placed before them she held back. Lobster omelette and shrimp curry renewed her wish to protest, but again she checked herself. Then there came whitebait, the speciality of the Greenwich taverns, and she acquiesced to that.

Stewed quail was brought in by the smiling and scraping waiters and she longed to be able to tell them to take back such a superfluous luxury. She did indeed decline to eat any herself.

'But, Harriet, this is a time to eat, to drink, to be merry.'

'And why, sir?'

It was a daring question, since it might have seemed designed to provoke another and a more important one in return.

But Richard answered the direct query without a second thought.

'Oh, because I am freed of a great burden, of a terrible suspicion. And because I owe that freedom to you.'

'But, sir, you are not free of it.'

'Nonsense, nonsense. That dreadful Redderman will never haul me into his presence again.'

'I think he might, sir. He said as much.'

'He had to say something, just to keep himself in countenance.'

'No, I think not. I do not see Inspector Redderman as a person who would feel much need for that.'

'Everybody feels as much. Everybody, high or low.'

'Perhaps to some extent, sir. But there are those who know themselves well enough not to seek to justify an error by attacking the person who points it out. And I believe Mr Redderman is such a one. If he said to you, as he did in the clearest terms, that he might have to look at your defence again then he meant just that. And – And, sir, I cannot see now who else may have been responsible for your father's death. Be sure the Inspector is considering whether he ought to take you to the police office once more.'

'No, no. I won't believe it. And you shan't talk of it. This is an evening marked out from any other.'

And he leant forward and rang vigorously at the bell for yet more delicacies to be brought up.

In fact, however, the next course set before them was not as much of a delicacy as stewed quail or curried shrimps. It was a joint of honest mutton.

Miss Unwin saw no reason to protest against that. She allowed Richard to carve for her, and even when he put a truly monstrous slice on her plate she cut a piece from it cheerfully and ate.

'Well, sir,' she said, 'this is a great deal better than the first piece of mutton you and I ate at the same table.'

She saw in her mind's eye that first dinner at the Harrow Road house with old Mr Partington grudging every mouthful that she and Richard, Captain Fulcher and Cousin Cornelia and the twins consumed.

'Why, yes,' Richard answered, 'this tastes very different from those appalling joints Mrs Meggs managed to buy for us, when she was not buying for my father alone.'

'Oh, I think, sir, to do her justice, she bought meat as cheaply for him as for any of us. I often wondered at the odd taste –'

She came to an abrupt halt.

'The odd taste,' she repeated slowly. 'The odd taste and – And what was it Vilkins called it? Yes, Cor Rosy Subjec' Mate.'

'What on earth are you saying? Vilkins, who is Vilkins? And what in heaven's name is Cor Rosy whatever it was you said?'

'That last, sir, is simply enough answered. It is Corrosive Sublimate.'

'I'm little the wiser. What is Corrosive Sublimate?'

'Why, of course, a gentleman would hardly know. But it is a liquid much used to keep floors and suchlike sweet. It kills offensive odours.'

Slowly a look of understanding grew on Richard's face.

'Kills offensive odours,' he repeated at last. 'On cheap tainted meat, you suggest?'

'Yes, sir, I do. I suggest that Mrs Meggs in her ignorance and her parsimony used Corrosive Sublimate to make the tainted meat she bought for a few pence palatable. And that is why your father, who ate meat more often than any of us, was so often ill. Why, you yourself once tried to persuade him to allow me meat. If he had agreed I might have become as ill. I am sure that in the end was why your father died.'

'But how can you be so sure?'

'The symptoms,' Miss Unwin said. 'The symptoms fit the bill exactly.'

'But how on earth do you know that? Isn't it mere wishful thinking?'

'No, sir, it is not. Corrosive Sublimate is chemically mercury bichloride. If taken, its effects are notably similar to those of arsenic poisoning. So Doctor Sumsion can be excused for his diagnosis.'

She laughed a little.

'What mercury bichloride does,' she went on with recaptured earnestness, 'is produce gastric disorder with inflammation of the gums giving a characteristic blue-black line. And, sir, I noticed just such blueness on your father's gums the day I had to tell him how I had come to see his hoard of gold.'

'And this is in that professor's book? The one you told Doctor Sumsion you had read for my sake?'

'Yes, sir, it is the words of Professor Potherton himself.

197

But I read them only this morning when I thought I ought to consult the book again.'

'But then, Harriet, we must telegraph Inspector Redderman immediately.'

And that was an extravagance which Miss Unwin did not feel inclined to forbid Richard Partington.

Chapter Twenty

After the telegraph message had been despatched and the rest of the gigantic meal offered by the Trafalgar had been more or less disposed of, out on the iron balcony above the swift-flowing moonlit Thames Richard Partington did at last put the question to Harriet Unwin she had known was sooner or later to come.

But she did not in a moment of fervent delight give him that answer 'Yes' which she had without any doubts foreseen of herself when once she knew that Richard was finally cleared of the shadow that had rested over him. Something prevented her, something deep in her mind which she found hard to pin down.

Surely, she told herself, the mystery of old Mr Partington's death is a mystery no more. Surely that cloud, which once in my lack of faith I almost believed must hang over Richard, surely it has now for ever dispersed.

Yet, despite all this, when she gave him his answer it was not one of unambiguous assent.

'Sir,' she said, 'I know that I owe you much. I would wish, too, no maidenly modesty to delay my answering you. But – Sir, may I have the space of a day, of twenty-four exact hours from this moment, before I give you my reply.'

Richard did look, in the strong moonlight, a little put out at this. But he paused hardly a moment before he spoke.

'Yes. Yes, of course. Yes, you shall have longer if you wish.'

'No, sir. I will not ask for one half-hour more. But – But, I know not why, I must have that amount of time before I do make my answer.'

So it was a much less jocose pair who made their way back in the threshing paddle-steamer to London Bridge and by fleet, rattling hansom to the Harrow Road house and their beds.

In hers, to her surprise, Miss Unwin fell at once into a deep, deep slumber.

She was awakened from it next morning, rather earlier than her usual hour, by Vilkins hammering thumpingly on her door and thrusting her head, capless, inside.

'Vilkins, why, what is it?'

'It's 'im, Unwin. It's 'im.'

'Who, him? It – It isn't Richard?'

The idea of some terrible catastrophe came into Miss Unwin's mind.

'Well, yes. Yes, it is the Master. And it aint.'

'Vilkins, pull yourself together. What has happened?'

'It's the Inspector, Unwin. That Mr Redderman. An' 'e wants your precious Richard again.'

Miss Unwin felt the tension flow out of her.

'Well, and have you told Mr Partington that he is wanted?'

'No. No, I daresn't. I come up to you straight away.'

'Then you must go down and wake the Master. Straight away.'

Then Miss Unwin relented.

'And, Vilkins, dear . . .'

'Yes?'

'It's all right. Everything's all right. Inspector Redderman will be coming to tell the Master just exactly that. Last night we hit on what it was that had been poisoning old Mr Partington. It was Corrosive Sublimate, Vilkins. Mrs Meggs had been using it to take the smell from tainted meat. That was all. Corrosive Sublimate by mistake.'

'Cor Rosy Subjec' Mate. Well, I never 'eard o' that used for meat.'

'And I hope you never do. Now, go and wake the Master.'

Vilkins went.

And in ten minutes Richard and Miss Unwin together faced the once formidable Inspector.

'Well, sir,' he said, 'I have telegraphed Professor Potherton – you know his reputation, I believe, Miss – and his answer is clear as a bell. The symptoms are all in accord with the regular administration of small quantities of Corrosive Sublimate, and his investigations confirm that decease can be attributed to that cause without a shadow of doubt. May I congratulate you, sir?'

'It is Miss Unwin whom you should congratulate, Inspector. Without her resolute study of a subject that a woman should not be asked to know about we should none of us have ever had the answer to the riddle of my father's death.'

Inspector Redderman considered this for a moment. Then he spoke.

'Yes, sir,' he said, 'I believe you may be quite right. Without Miss Unwin here and her endeavours the mystery might have remained just that for ever.'

He gave Miss Unwin a self-contained little bob of a bow, bade farewell and was seen at the house in the Harrow Road no more.

Miss Unwin and Richard Partington stood where they had listened to him, in the bright and newly furnished drawing room, in long silence. Both, it seemed, were too overwhelmed by this final and definite end to their fears to have a word to say.

Perhaps Richard remained for even longer in that stunned state. But Miss Unwin did not. Gradually her powers of thought had come back to her in all their old full force. She considered her situation as it had now come to be.

And she found she had come to a certain conclusion.

'Sir,' she said, when she had looked at that conclusion up and down in her mind. 'Sir, last night you asked me a question, and I begged you for a period of twenty-four hours to consider my answer.'

'I did, I did,' Richard said, coming out of his stupefied reverie with a start.

'Well, sir, I feel able to give you my answer now.'

Richard's round face lit up.

'Then – Then, Harriet, you will?'

'No, sir,' said Harriet Unwin. 'I will not.'

'Not? Not? But I don't think I understand. Are you saying – can you be saying that – that you will not marry me?'

Miss Unwin gave a deep, deep sigh.

'It is what I must say,' she answered.

'Must? But I see no must. Why? Why cannot you marry me? It is the dearest wish of my heart.'

'Yes, sir. I know that to be so.'

'Then why, Harriet? Why? Why? Why?'

'You wish me to tell you? It will not be the most pleasant hearing.'

'I must know. I must.'

'Very well then, sir. I cannot marry you because in doing so I would tie myself for ever to a man who is – I have known this for longer than I have been prepared to admit even to myself – to a man who is an incurable spendthrift. Oh, sir, I know that you have every excuse. Your father's impossible miserliness must have driven you to the other extreme. But that is where you are, sir. I have hoped, without quite knowing I was hoping, that after a while you would show signs of moderation. That – that your wild extravagance would prove only temporary. But it is not. You, sir, know it, do you not?'

Richard Partington was pale as a man of ivory. But he slowly lowered his head.

'Yes. Yes, you are right. Now I have money that I can

spend I shall spend it,' he said. 'I know that I should not. I knew yesterday when I ordered that great feast at Greenwich that it was something that I ought not to be doing. But I did it. I did it.'

There were tears, bright tears, now in his eyes.

'Harriet, Miss Unwin,' he said, 'I know you are right. I cannot, I must not, lay claim to you. It – It is time for us to part, is it not?'

There were tears, too, in Miss Unwin's eyes.

'Yes, sir,' she said, 'it is time for us to part.'